Bob Moats

I0567269

Doyle's Haunting

Rev. 1012141030a

Doyle's Haunting

For information and address:
Magic 1 Productions
P.O. Box 524, Fraser MI 48026-0524
Website: http://murdernovels.com
Cover by Bob Moats

Extra special thanks to:

Special thanks to Susan Haughton who edited this book and for her great suggestions.

Thanks to the beta readers Cindy Gross Valstad, Al Norris, Bill Sandy, Carolyn Linington, Rebecca Hester, Janet Lawson, Sherry Tull, Fleur Wilkinson, Deborah Gauze, and Amy Morningstar

Thank you to all the people who purchased this book. I hope you enjoy it as much as I enjoyed writing it for my faithful readers.

The Jim Richards Family of Readers is listed in the back of the book.

Doyle's Haunting by Bob Moats

Chapter 1

Marge was thumbing through a scandal magazine at her desk in the office of Doyle and Drew Investigations. She grinned as Oscar Drew came over to drop off some reports he had finished for cases he recently closed. Mostly spousal cheating cases that he enjoyed following. They weren't difficult cases, mostly sneaking around photographing men or women cheating on their spouses.

"Marge, do you really read those trashy things?" Oscar asked Marge when he saw the tabloid in her hands.

"Oh, Oscar. I don't believe anything they print, but it's fun to read about all the scandals going on. They're so silly, they can't be real."

"I've skimmed a few of them. My second wife was obsessed by them. She believed whatever they printed. I was glad when she divorced me. I finally burned all the tabloids she collected."

"I like the stories about the odd creatures around the country. Big Foot in upper Michigan, unicorns in Florida, monkey boys living in a shelter in Maine. It's all so funny."

"Glad you find it funny and not real. It's the people out there that believe that crap that worries me. If they believe that, then they'll believe anything," Oscar said, moving back to his desk.

"This story is about the ghosts haunting the mansions of Detroit. It's a Halloween special and they say murders have happened frequently." Marge said.

"Marge, there have never been any real reports of ghosts harming humans. The humans hurt themselves running from what they believed were ghosts."

"I know, Oscar. But it's fun to read about them." Marge said.

"Read about what?" Doyle asked coming over from the back of the office, where he was rummaging through the storage space.

"Monsters and ghosts," Marge said.

"Where?" Doyle asked.

Doyle's Haunting

"Everywhere. This article is about Detroit. There are ghost houses that have been frightening people for years."

"I don't believe in ghosts," Doyle said. "There has never been any real proof that they exist. Lots of people say they have photographed supposed ghosts, but all they had was poor photography and lens flares. If there were real ghosts, they'd take over the world and not just hide in houses, haunting them."

"Ah, a skeptic. If you saw a ghost, would you believe then?" Oscar asked.

"If I saw a ghost, I'd have to investigate it. To substantiate that it's real and not a hoax or a hallucination."

"When was the last time you hallucinated?" Oscar asked.

"I can't discuss that. It was in the sixties and everyone was doing it," Doyle said with a coy smile.

"You were a pot-head? I'm amazed," Oscar laughed.

"I wasn't a pot-head, thank you. Yes, I experimented with certain substances, but only once. Well, maybe twice. There was this girl in Detroit and…"

"Say no more. If a girl was involved, you would have smoked straw," Oscar laughed.

"Let's drop it. Don't you have a case to solve?"

"I do and I'm going out now to get on it. Another cheating spouse. You know we're getting quite a reputation for finding evidence of philandering."

"It's the new divorce attorneys I talked to. As much as I dislike them, they keep us busy. They send their clients to us to follow their husbands or wives and we reap the rewards of income."

"Speaking of income, what did you do with the money that Dante gave back to you from your stay in paradise?"

"I sent it to Lorna. She needed to get back on her feet after her husband's murder," Doyle replied.

"That was very nice of you, Arthur," Marge said hearing him.

"Well, we put the poor woman through hell on the island. It was the least we could do for her. Now can we get back to business?"

Marge giggled and picked up her magazine. Oscar picked up his camera bag and said he was going. Doyle sat at his desk thinking about what he was going to do. The back door opened and Doyle turned, thinking it was Oscar forgetting something. It was Poppy Drake, Doyle's girlfriend.

"Ah, slipping in the back door now?" Doyle smiled.

"I realized that I didn't need to keep coming in through the front door. That's a long walk around the building from the back parking lot."

"I wondered why you kept doing that."

"Hi Margie, how's life after our adventure in paradise?" Poppy said, referring to their trip to the Hawaiian islands, that resulted in a couple murders.

"Nice and quiet," Marge replied. "I even have TV again. You never know how much you miss creature comforts until they're gone. My next vacation will be somewhere there are lots of people having fun."

"I could send you to Las Vegas. There are lots of people having fun."

"I'll consider it. After I save some money," Marge said.

Doyle turned to Poppy as she moved close to him. She leaned down and kissed his lips. "That's a nice way to start the day," Doyle said.

Poppy sat on the chair next to his desk and crossed her beautiful legs. That always distracted Doyle.

"What's up?" he asked, coming out of his thoughts of her legs.

"My company is sending me out to investigate a hotel in Detroit. They claim that a guest was injured by a ghost and they need to cover medical costs."

Doyle looked at Marge when Poppy brought up the ghost subject. If Marge was listening, she wasn't showing it. "Your company covers injuries by ghosts? Do all insurance companies have provisions for that?"

"No, but it's covered under bodily injuries on premises. They say the reason is that the guest claims to have been pushed down the stairs by an apparition of an old woman."

"I'd say you have a tough case. The ghost is probably hiding now, so you have to believe the injured woman as to whom the ghost was. Are you going to interrogate the ghost?"

"If I can find it. That's why I came here. I'd like you to come along to help find the ghost."

Doyle's Haunting

"Poppy, my dear, I've already discussed this with Marge and Oscar, not more than ten minutes ago. I don't believe in ghosts."

"That's why I want you to go. You are skeptical of most things and you can balance my feelings about spirits."

"Are you saying you believe?"

"I had an experience with a ghost in my youth, yes."

Doyle looked to Marge who was now listening intently. "Did you get that, Marge? We have a real ghost story here. Shall we sit by a campfire and talk of spirits and monsters?"

"Stop making fun. It happened to me and I never forgot it. I was young, but not stupid. And I did see a ghost in my grandparent's house late at night. She came into the room I was staying in overnight and stood staring at me. I couldn't move as she came closer and pointed at me. She moaned and then disappeared. I never knew why she came into the room or why she pointed at me."

"Maybe it was her room and she didn't like you being in it. Ghosts are very territorial from what I hear."

"Maybe so, but I'm not going after a ghost without backup. I figured you were big and strong and could protect me from an old lady ghost."

Doyle sat staring at her, then said, "Marge, hold my calls, I'm going ghost hunting."

*

Chapter 2

"Where are we going?" Doyle asked as he got into his cherry red Dodge Charger.

Poppy slid in the passenger seat and said, "The old Algonquin Hotel on Cass."

"I thought they closed that place down years ago."

"They did, but some company bought it and renovated it. They now have a nice place from what I hear, but there have been stories of a ghost haunting the building. It got worse when the construction was going on. Lights kept going on and off and tools seemed to be moved around when the men weren't looking."

"Poor wiring and careless workers not paying attention to their tools. That's all, no ghosts. Did the workers say they saw any spooks?"

"Not really, which is why I'm skeptical about this injury claim. I'm surprised the injured woman didn't claim she tripped on a rug and fell down the stairs. I was told she insisted that she heard a noise behind her and turned her head to see what it was. She said an old woman in black was standing right behind her, so close it frightened her. She turned and fell down the flight of stairs. She broke her arm and bruised a few ribs."

"Was she sure it wasn't another guest at the hotel who ran away when she realized she frightened the victim?"

"That's what I want to find out. The victim is still in the hotel, they are letting her stay until she feels better."

"Well, I might fall down some stairs if I could get free room and board," Doyle said with a laugh. "Oh and I heard from Lorna. She called me yesterday to thank us for the money. She's trying to start over now after her husband's murder on the island."

"That's good. I was worried for her," Poppy replied.

They arrived at the hotel and pulled into the parking structure next to the building. Doyle parked and they went to the entrance. The lobby was what they used to call opulent. Gaudy was what Doyle was thinking. The original building was over a century old and had many dignitaries and celebrities staying there. It was said that President Teddy Roosevelt liked to stay there if he came into the city. The building was hit hard by the Depression, and the neighborhood was becoming run down. Crime was plaguing the area, so many potential guests stayed away.

"They did a nice job restoring it to the original condition. Lots of gold and deco giving it a feel of a special place to stay," Doyle said.

"It looks spooky to me," Poppy said. "It looks like something out of *The Shining* with Jack Nicholson. I don't think I'd stay here."

"You're just a modern girl. I enjoyed the past growing up in a small town up north. I appreciated the old buildings of Detroit when I first came here to work for the police. Too bad they're tearing most of them down to put up glass and chrome buildings. Now this building I can appreciate."

Doyle's Haunting

"Well, you can have it. Now I have to find a Mr. Roderick Hallsey. He's the general manager of this haunted house."

"Roderick Hallsey, he even sounds like an old time manager. I wonder if he has dark circles under his eyes and a pale colored face."

Poppy stopped a bellboy and asked where the manager's office was. He smiled at her. Doyle figured he was probably undressing her in his filthy young mind. The young man told her where to go and then went off.

"He looks to be about fifteen. I guess they hire youngsters for the less important jobs," Doyle said.

"There are child labor laws about that. I'm sure he's old enough to work here," Poppy said, as she made her way to the office. The door had a brass plate attached to it saying it was the manager's office. Below that was a small printed sign saying to come in. They did.

The office was small, filled with boxes and assorted junk probably left over from the original hotel. At the back of the mess was a desk and there sat a smallish balding man with large round glasses. He looked up and was surprised to see people in his office.

"May I help you?" he said nervously.

Poppy went to his desk and held her hand out. "I'm Poppy Drake from American Causality and Life. I'm here to investigate the injury claim you filed."

"Oh, yes, thank you for coming. I suppose you'll need to talk to Mrs. Winfield, the poor lady who fell. She's up in her room, resting."

Doyle thought that she was probably bouncing on the bed, enjoying her free stay. He looked around the room at the many potted plants and signs that were from the hotel years ago. Some had directions to a gym and a pool, one was for a spa. There were posters from old movies that the local theatres ran back in the thirties.

"Yes, I'd like to talk to her and then see the spot where this accident happened." Poppy asked.

"Was it an accident, or was she deliberately pushed down the stairs? I'd say it was attempted murder. That poor woman could have broken her neck and expired right there."

"That's being a bit dramatic, wouldn't you say." Poppy questioned.

"I'm sorry, I have an active imagination. I write scripts for televisions shows," he said beaming.

"Really? What shows?" Doyle asked.

Doyle's Haunting

"Oh, none on TV right now. I submit my scripts to the producers and I wait for them to call me."

Doyle was realizing this man probably has a few acorns rolling around in his head.

"That's good. Now, may we see Mrs. Winfield?" Poppy asked.

"Oh, uh, sure. I'll take you to her," he said and stood. The man had to have been just under five feet tall. He came around his desk and went out of the room, followed by Poppy and Doyle.

"Peter, what are you doing here? You're supposed to help Mr. Allan with his exercises," Hallsey said to another young man in a hotel uniform standing in the lobby.

"I was just on my way, Mr. Hallsey," he said and rushed off.

"I have to keep on top of these men or they just goof off." Hallsey continued to an old wire cage elevator and entered. He waited for Poppy and Doyle, but Doyle stood back.

"What's the matter?" Poppy asked him.

"What floor is Winfield on?" Doyle asked Hallsey.

"This elevator is entirely safe, sir," he replied.

"I know. I just like stairs better. Now, what floor?"

"Four, we'll meet you there," he replied.

Poppy entered and grinned at Doyle as he headed to the stairs. "He's not fond of confined spaces," she told Hallsey.

"Ah, I see," he replied.

Doyle watched them go up in the cage as he climbed the stairs. Poppy waved to him on each floor until they came to the fourth floor. Hallsey pulled back the metal gate and motioned for Poppy to exit. Doyle came up and said, "That climb was invigorating."

"This way, please," Hallsey said and they followed. They came to a door and Hallsey took out his passkey and unlocked the door.

"Doesn't she mind you just walking in?" Doyle asked.

"No, she says it's fine."

"Mrs. Winfield?" Hallsey called out.

They heard her call out, "Roderick! Get in here. That damn ghost has been back!"

*

Chapter 3

"What happened?" Hallsey asked in a panic as he went into the bedroom. Mrs. Winfield was prone on her bed covered by a big comforter.

"Roderick, the ghost is messing with my room. I woke this morning and the curtains were drawn shut. I dozed back off and when I awoke, the curtains were opened."

"Mrs. Winfield, the curtains were opened by housekeeping. I told them to freshen your room and open the curtains each morning. It wasn't the ghost."

"Oh, well, it could have been. I can hear her in the night moaning. She is crying for a lost love. I just know it."

Winfield turned to Poppy and Doyle. "It's an old legend about a woman who found her lover murdered in one of the rooms. The police never caught the killer."

"When did this happen?" Poppy asked.

"Late in 1945, around the time the big war was starting to come to an end when the Japanese surrendered. The woman was so desolate without her lover, she hung herself in the room where her lover was murdered. It was a messy scandal, and the manager at the time tried to keep it contained. But the press made a big splash out of it. The hotel took another hit. Not as bad as during the Depression, but bad enough to lose business. After a while it got so bad that they couldn't pay the staff and they closed the doors October 29th, 1946. Two days before Halloween."

"Spooky," Doyle said quietly to Poppy. She hit him in the stomach with the back of her hand.

"Mrs. Winfield, this is a lady from the insurance company, she needs to talk to you about your accident."

"Accident, hell. That ghost woman pushed me down the stairs. I could have been killed."

"That's what I told her, but she has to confirm your story before the insurance people will pay for your recovery."

Doyle's Haunting

The woman looked at Poppy from the bed and said, "What more do you need to know? I was pushed by a ghost."

"I understand, Mrs. Winfield. How did you determine it was a ghost?" Poppy asked.

"You're too pretty to be an insurance investigator. And your partner there, he's a hunk."

Doyle tried not to laugh aloud, only snorted a little. Poppy gave him a quick warning glance.

"Thank you, Mrs. Winfield, but how did you know the woman was a ghost?"

"She was pale and almost transparent. I think she was floating a little. She definitely looked dead."

"Did you recognize her?"

"Nope, have no idea who she was. But I think she looked a little like that woman in the painting in the lobby."

"That's just a painting that the owners put up for decoration, Mrs. Winfield." Hallsey explained. "She's no one important."

"Well I think she looked like her, now that I think of it."

"But you didn't recognize her as a real human being?" Poppy asked.

"No, she was a ghost," she insisted.

Poppy looked at Doyle. He shrugged. She said, "Thank you Mrs. Winfield. We have a little more examining to do and then I'll have my report ready for my company." She turned and went towards the door, followed by Doyle and Hallsey.

In the hallway, Poppy asked to see the accident site.

"Of course, follow me, please." He walked away as they followed the little man.

"Mrs. Winfield seems to be very outspoken and loud," Poppy said to Hallsey.

"She's a bossy person and, yes, loud. She screams at the staff and is never happy. If it weren't for her lawyers, I would have booted her out long ago. You were lucky, she seemed to be in a good mood today."

"Good mood?" Doyle said. "Nice."

They arrived at the top of the stairs on the floor. Hallsey stopped just before the edge. "This is where she stood when she was pushed."

Doyle's Haunting

Poppy looked around the area and stood at the top of the stairs, about where Mrs. Winfield probably stood before her tumble down the stairs.

She studied the carpeting and the handrail. She looked down the slope and figured a fall would cause bodily harm.

"Maybe if the owners would put in thicker carpeting, softer nap, then perhaps others wouldn't be harmed falling down the stairs," she said.

"I'll recommend that. Frankly, I think she was clumsy and tripped. But her lawyers advised her to sue if she didn't get satisfaction. I'm hoping your company can cover the cost for this fiasco."

"I'm putting in my report that she stumbled on the flimsy carpet. Look here." She pointed to a portion of loose carpeting. "I'll try to help you with recompense but it won't cover all of her stay here. You'll have to deal with that. This was not a deliberate attempt to do her bodily harm, but as you said, she was clumsy."

"Yes, I'll deal with it. I have to answer to the board of directors of the hotel. I'm not looking forward to that."

"You have a board of directors?" Doyle asked.

"Yes, this is a corporation and they have the bigwigs running it. Well, they don't actually run it, I do. They just collect the rewards of income."

He didn't sound happy. Poppy stood away from the stairs. "When did this accident happen?"

"Early in the morning, around eight, as she was coming down for breakfast in the dining room."

"Was it dark then?"

"No, our lights were on as they are now."

"Mr. Hallsey, be honest with me. Do you believe a ghost could have committed this?"

"Miss Drake, I've experienced many strange things in my three years here. I wasn't a believer, but now I'm not sure. I've experienced things that tested my religious upbringing."

"Don't most religions support life after death? Heaven, hell, and purgatory where the dead are stuck before they can leave this existance. Haunting the earth. If you believe in religion, then you'd have to believe in ghosts, right?"

Hallsey paused and was thinking. "Your explanation isn't quite correct, but I guess you could say that. I believe in angels and the hereafter, so I guess there would be ghosts wandering around."

Doyle's Haunting

"Well, I can't put in my report that a ghost committed this. It's bad enough I'm the only woman investigator in the company, I don't want to be laughed out," Poppy said. "This carpet being loose can be a reason for her falling. Your hotel may have to put up with higher premiums, until you can fix the carpets."

"I guess that's the best I can hope for. I'll let the higher ups know."

"You don't mind if we look around? Maybe find your ghost?" Poppy asked.

"No, explore all you'd like. I hope you find a ghost. It will make me feel better," Hallsey said.

"Okay, we won't keep you any longer. Thank you for the tour. We'll see ourselves out."

Hallsey gave them a weak smile and went down the stairs.

"So what do you think?" Poppy asked of Doyle.

"I'd say you have a crazy old lady with high priced lawyers, taking advantage of the hotel. I don't think she saw a ghost. She was probably on medication and hallucinated. Did you see all the drug bottles on her side table?"

"I did. I didn't want to push the issue, but she did seem to be lethargic. Although feisty. If she saw a ghost, I'd say she was hallucinating when she fell."

*

Chapter 4

"So, where shall we start?" Poppy asked.

"Let's see if there's an attic. Ghosts love to hide in attics." Doyle turned as a bellboy came up the stairs. "Excuse me, what's your name?"

"Andrew, sir."

"Well, Andrew, do you know where the attic is?"

The young man looked surprised by the request and said, "I don't know, I've never been up there. I'm still fairly new here, so I haven't found all the places there are in this building. There is a door at the end of the fifth floor that's locked, maybe that's the way up."

"The fifth floor is the top floor?" Doyle asked. The young man nodded. "Thanks, we'll check it out and let you know."

Doyle's Haunting

The young man went off and Doyle turned to Poppy. "Shall we hit the fifth floor?"

"Lead the way, stair climber," she said with a smile.

They went up the stairs to the fifth floor and looked for a door at the end of the hall, they found it. They went to it and Doyle tried the knob.

"Yep, it's locked," Doyle said.

"I can see that, so open it," Poppy replied.

"Why do you think I can do something illegal like picking a lock?"

"Because you've done it before."

"Oh, right. Well then, stand back." He pulled a small wallet from his jacket and selected a couple lock picks.

"Do you always carry those?" Poppy asked.

"Sure, I'm a certified locksmith."

"Since when?"

"I bought it online. You can get a lot of certifications if you just look." He made a quick turn on it and the lock gave away. "See, I come in handy."

"Now to catch our ghost," Poppy said ominously. "You go first."

"Chicken."

"Hey, I've already seen a ghost. You have to be anointed. So take a walk," she said.

"If I get attacked by a ghost, will you save me?" he asked.

"Hell, no. I'll be running to save my life," she replied.

"Thanks," Doyle said and they went through the door.

They climbed up a short flight of stairs. The place was dark, but light was coming in through a couple dirty skylights. It was dusty smelling and there were spider webs attached to numerous beams above.

"I hate spiders more than ghosts," Poppy said. "If one drops down, you'll kill it, won't you?"

"Hell, no. I'll be running to save my life," Doyle mimicked her.

Doyle's Haunting

"Stop that. I'm serious. I need to be spider-free, so if you see one, kill it."

"Shall I use my gun?"

"Whatever works, just take that sucker down. Now let's find our ghost." She turned and went into the room. It was filled with junk, boxes, old furniture and a moose.

Poppy jumped back, running into Doyle, when she found the moose. "My God, what is a stuffed moose doing up here?"

"I'm wondering how they got it up here. The horns are so big they shouldn't be able to fit through the door."

"Whatever, it's strange. Maybe Teddy Roosevelt shot it and brought it here. I heard he stayed here a couple times."

Doyle was listening to her talk as he scouted the attic. "I don't see any ghosts in this mess. Maybe they like cleaner quarters." He studied the floor and said, "Someone has been up here. Humans, not ghosts. Look at the dust on the floor, it's been disturbed by feet."

"I saw that. They go to that door," she said pointing to a door on one wall. Doyle went to it and tried the knob.

Poppy came up and asked, "Can't you open it?"

"No, it's locked. But there's no lock on the door, it must be latched from the other side. Strange."

"It's ghost central. They can float through the door while everyone else has to say the secret word to open the door."

"I doubt that spoken words could open this door. The footprints go in, but don't come out. Now that's weird."

"Well, break it in."

Doyle tapped on the door then said, "This is a solid oak door, probably very thick. I'd only break my shoulder if I attacked it." He studied the door frame and it was not going to move.

"Well, if something is in there, I want to know." Poppy insisted.

Doyle knocked on the door.

"What are you doing?" Poppy asked.

"If someone is in there, maybe they'll answer."

Doyle's Haunting

"If someone is in there, I don't want to know. Maybe a serial killer lives up here."

"I'm sure you'll shoot him. You do have your .38?"

"Ever since you bought it for me, I can't seem to leave home without it."

"Good, someday you'll save my life with it. Just not today, I hope." He knocked again.

They heard a crashing noise from the other side of the door. They both jumped back and stared.

"I heard that. There's someone in there," Poppy said.

They listened, then heard a cat meowing. "Ha! It was a cat," Doyle said breathing again.

"Great, but how did it get in there?" Poppy asked.

"Maybe there's a broken window in there. There could be a colony of cats hiding out."

"Do cats attack?"

"Only if you're opening a can of cat food," Doyle said with a grin. "Well, I don't know how we can get in there. I'll talk to Hallsey, and see what he can do to get us in."

They heard another crash and jumped. "I think we're done up here. Shall we go?" Poppy said.

"Coward. But just for you, we'll leave," Doyle said. "Shall we go see if there's a basement?"

Poppy didn't reply, she just left Doyle alone. She was out the door as Doyle kicked the mystery door, just to shake up the cat. There was another crash, and Doyle scooted out of the attic.

After Doyle left, the mystery door slowly opened a crack, then slammed back shut.

Hallsey was at the check-in desk smiling at new guests signing in. Poppy and Doyle held back until they were finished. On command the bellboy came, took their bags and led them to their room.

Doyle and Poppy went to the counter and waited until Hallsey finished filling out the register. He looked to them and said, "Did you find anything?"

"We got into the attic and found a door that is locked from the other side. What's the deal?" Doyle asked.

"Oh, you were up there?" He looked surprised. "Well, that door was sealed many years ago. There was a man hiding up there and he turned out to be a serial murderer. The police finally found him, and when they went up there, they found that he stored his bodies in the attic in containers filled with lye. The room was sealed off after it was cleaned out. I haven't been in there, as it is sealed."

"The press never heard about that?" Doyle asked.

"Oh they did, but it was hushed up for some reason. I think the killer was a relation to the owner of the newspaper back then."

"This hotel has had its share of murders and death. I'm surprised the new owners re-opened the place with its history." Doyle said.

"Mr. Doyle, yes, this hotel has had its share of death. A number of times and that's why I have to believe there are ghosts haunting the place."

*

Chapter 5

"Mr. Hallsey, I really think we'll need to get into that locked room. My insurance company will demand to know that there are no dangerous items in there that could cause harm to the hotel or the guests. It could void your policy with my company and you'd be without liability insurance."

Hallsey looked upset. "I don't know how to get in there. I'll see if there's someone in the corporation who can open it. The construction company who renovated the hotel couldn't get into the room."

"Well, either you open it or I'll have someone come in who can," she said with a side glance to Doyle. He cleared his throat. "I'm serious, you have a policy that covers the whole building. If the room is dangerous, we can cancel your coverage."

Doyle had a feeling she was bluffing, just to get in the room. He didn't challenge her, he wanted to see inside the room also.

"Oh, dear. I'll make some calls and see what can be done," he said.

"Good, now can you point us to your basement?" Poppy asked.

Doyle's Haunting

"Oh, you want to go in the basement, too?"

"We do."

"Uh, I'll have one of the boys show you the way. All that's down there is the laundry room, where we clean the linens, and janitorial supplies."

"That's fine. We'd still like to see it."

He mumbled, "I knew Winfield would bite me." He called for a bellboy and one came running. It was Andrew, the boy who told them where the attic was.

"Andrew, take these people to the basement, carefully, please."

"Yes, sir," Andrew replied. "Follow me, please." He turned and went off, followed by Doyle and Poppy.

"Andrew, the attic is behind the door on the fifth floor. But don't go up there. Unless you want to face the ghosts," Doyle joked with the young man.

Andrew stopped and turned and said, "You've seen the ghosts? I thought I was the only one."

Doyle and Poppy stood waiting for the young man to continue. "I saw a ghost in the hallway of the fifth floor last month, just after I started working

34

here. Scared the crap out of me. Sorry ma'am, it frightened me. But I needed the job so I kept quiet about it."

"What exactly did you see?" Poppy asked.

"Well, it was an old woman, all in black and pale looking, standing at the end of the hallway by that attic door. She pointed at me and screamed. I was shocked and ran down the stairs. I've been afraid to go back up there alone."

Poppy looked at Doyle. "Old woman in black. Sound familiar?"

"Yes, but on the wrong floor to push Winfield. Unless the ghost is wandering," Doyle replied.

"Thank you Andrew," Poppy said. "We won't tell anyone about your sighting."

"Thanks, but a few of the other hotel staff have seen her too. She haunts the fifth floor."

"Was this in daylight or night time?"

"I saw her after eight at night. It was getting dark up there, they hadn't turned on the lights yet. Daylight savings time, you know. There was no one staying in the rooms up there at that time, so lights weren't needed. Cost of electricity, you know. I was up there because Hallsey said to check and see if the lights were on yet. He controls the lights. After I saw her, I ran back down and told Hallsey they weren't on. He turned them on again and wanted me to go back up to see if the lights were on. I just went to the bottom of the stairs on the fourth floor and could see the lights were on. So I told him they were. But I didn't go back up there."

"Thank you Andrew. That helps a lot. Okay, take us to the basement." Poppy said.

Poppy said quietly to Doyle as they followed the young man, "We need to see inside the mystery room. I think there's something more to this."

"I agree." Doyle said. "We need to come back tomorrow and insist that we get in."

Andrew opened a door next to a service elevator. "These are the stairs going down to the basement. The elevator is for housekeeping to bring linen baskets, and cleaning carts up from the basement where they have the janitorial supplies."

"Andrew, do you really believe in ghosts?" Poppy asked.

"I didn't, until I saw her."

"Do you know who she is?" Doyle asked.

"They say she was a woman who hung herself because someone murdered her lover. It was in a room on the fifth floor. They don't allow guests to use that room."

"Does she often haunt the hotel?"

"Only when the moon is full. They say her lover was murdered under a full moon."

"I thought that was werewolves and full moons?" Doyle said.

"Yeah, but this was different. I don't believe in werewolves," Andrew replied. "She comes out and walks the floors at night but only when it's dark up there. Mr. Hallsey tries to be sure the lights are on early during the full moon."

"Hallsey knows she roams the floor?"

"He hasn't seen her, but he believes she's there."

"Thank you, Andrew. We can go downstairs by ourselves," Poppy said.

Andrew turned and walked away from them. "Shall we go down into the pit of hell?" Poppy said with a weak smile.

Doyle's Haunting

"Lead the way. This is your investigation. I'm just along to scream when we see a ghost," Doyle grinned.

"My big brave savior. I knew I could depend on you," she said as she went in and down the stairs. The stairwell was not well lit, so Poppy was careful going down. "Is it just me, or is this place spooky all over?" she asked Doyle as he was trying not to trip on the narrow steps.

"Oh, by the way, I heard from the contractor who was building your new cabin. He's pretty much done with it," Poppy said.

"Well, that was quick. I guess since the old cabin was burned down to ashes, it was easy to rebuild. We'll have to go up soon and take a look."

"I look forward to it. I'd like to sit by the lake and fish," Poppy said as she continued down the stairs.

"You fish? I hate fishing. I feel sorry for the worm," he said as they reached the bottom floor.

She turned and smiled, "You're just a softy for small animals."

"Is a worm an animal?" Doyle asked.

"How should I know? I just fish with them, I don't talk to them."

"Do worms talk? That's scary."

Poppy didn't reply. It was useless to have an intelligent conversation with Doyle when he got goofy. She moved down a hallway and found a large laundry room with a number of washing machines and dryers. There were four women who looked to be Mexican working the machines and folding towels. One older, heavy set woman saw Poppy and Doyle and went to them.

"May I help you?" she asked.

"We're from the hotel's insurance company. We're just inspecting."

"Well, go ahead," she said, then turned to go back to her table to fold.

"Wait. May I ask you a question?" Poppy called to her. The woman returned to them. "Have you ever seen any ghosts down here?"

The woman's eyes went big and she crossed herself. "Mi Dios, don't talk of such things. Leave the spirits upstairs."

*

Chapter 6

The woman turned and left them. She spoke something in Spanish to the other women and they all gave Poppy and Doyle an evil eye.

"I think I'd rather face a ghost than those women," Doyle said quietly.

"Let's move on before we end up in a dryer."

They went past the laundry and down a short hallway to another large room. This one had janitorial carts and supplies to clean the building. There was no one in the room, other than one old man sitting at a desk looking at a newspaper. He turned his head to them and looked surprised.

"Well, why would such a beautiful woman be doing down in the dungeon?" he asked as she came over. He remained seated, then he pulled back and they could see he was in a wheelchair.

"Hello. And who might you be?" Poppy asked.

"I'm Herman. I'm in charge of the supplies down here. You can't take anything while I'm watching."

"Supplies?" Poppy asked.

"Yep, soap, detergent, floor wax, glass cleaner, toilet paper and all that sort of stuff. If I don't keep track of it all, the people in housekeeping would steal the hotel blind. So I ration it out."

"Very good, Herman. You're saving the hotel money that way."

"Better believe it, missy. I do a service. I've been here for over 30 years, since before they closed and then after they reopened."

"You've been here a long time. You must know a lot about the hotel then?"

"Yes, I do. I know everything," he said with a wink.

Poppy smiled. "Do you know about the ghost that haunts the fifth floor?"

He looked at her differently now, with a suspicious stare. "You ain't some reporter are you? I don't talk to reporters. They ruined the reputation of this place when they slammed the hotel about the murders and the woman who hanged herself. Got us closed up, they did."

Doyle's Haunting

"No, we're not reporters, we're investigators for the insurance company that covers this hotel. There's a woman up on the fourth floor who said she was pushed down the stairs by the ghost of a woman."

"Dang fool Winfield. She's a pain in the ass. The staff tells me tales about her and the bitching she does about everything. Now she's staying in that room until they pay her for her injuries."

"Well, that's why I'm here. To see if she's faking the story of her fall. What can you tell me about the ghost?"

"That's Jane Frobush. Early in 1946, she hung herself in room 504 after they found her lover dead in that same room late in 1945. He was murdered and his throat was slit from ear to ear. Poor old Jane went crazy after that and done herself in a couple months later on the full moon. They say she haunts every full moon now. The hotel tries to keep guests out of the fifth floor around that time. Luckily there are only five rooms up there. I don't know why they don't just close off that floor and let the ghost have it."

Poppy looked at Doyle and grinned. He frowned back at her. "I really would like to see this ghost," Doyle said.

"Well, next week there's a full moon, come stay and watch for her," the old man said.

"I may do that," Doyle said.

"You can stay by yourself," Poppy told him. "You take a picture of the ghost and then I'll believe it."

"Where does this basement go, Herman?" Doyle asked.

"Past here it's just storage. Mostly crap left over from years ago. They should have a rummage sale and clear it out. A lot of that stuff back there are antiques."

"Thanks, Herman. We'll go have a look," Doyle said and pushed Poppy towards the area.

"Maybe I don't want to go see antiques. This basement is dusty and smelly," she complained.

"Now I thought you were a bulldog when it came to your investigations. You're disappointing me," Doyle said to her.

"Grow up, ghost boy. There are things in my life that I don't care for, besides you. Musty old antiques are not high on my list of joy. You can go antiquing, or hitting garage sales, whatever, just don't ask me to go."

Doyle's Haunting

"Damn, there goes our Sunday drives in the country, stopping at quaint antique shops to buy an old writing desk owned by Ben Franklin."

"Why would I want a writing desk owned by Ben Franklin?" she asked.

"History, my dear. Sentimental keepsake, lots of reasons."

She smiled and said, "Doyle, you are the only antique I want in my life. You don't even smell musty. Now can we get back upstairs?"

"I'm not an antique yet. So don't rush me."

They went back and said good bye to Herman, then rushed past the Mexican ghost haters. They went up and back to the lobby where they found Mr. Hallsey talking to new guests. Andrew came by and took their luggage and led them to their room.

"Mr. Hallsey," Poppy said going to the man, "I need to ask you again to get us into the room in the attic."

"I put a call into the company that owns the hotel and was told they'd get back to me. That's the best I can do for now."

"I'll be back tomorrow and if you don't have someone here to open the door, we'll have to bring in someone who can. It's your choice. Let us in one way or another or lose your insurance. That would be disastrous for your company. Especially if your ghost hurts another guest."

Hallsey looked worried and said, "I'll get on it. If I mess up and lose our insurance, we'd have to close again. You were the only company that would insure us. I'd lose my job and I can't have that. I have to take care of my mother."

"Well, Roderick, we don't want your mother to be out on the street, do we?" Doyle offered.

"Goodness, no. I'll take care of it if I have to take a crowbar to the door," he said, frighten by the thought.

"Has anyone ever tried to open the door?" Poppy asked.

"When they were remodeling the hotel, a couple of construction workers tried to open the door. The supervisor came around and both men were passed out on the floor. Every attempt after that resulted in some kind of strange incident. They finally left it alone. The story of the ghost finally got to them and they stayed away from the door."

"This is getting stranger and stranger," Poppy said to Doyle. "Ghosts are getting annoying."

Doyle's Haunting

"Mr. Hallsey, we'll try and save you from losing your job. If you don't have someone in to open the door, we'll take care of it." Doyle said.

"Thank you, I don't want to tempt the fates," he said with a sigh of relief.

"Okay, we'll be back tomorrow," Poppy said. They left the lobby and went back out to the car.

Doyle got in behind the wheel and just sat there. "What's the matter?" Poppy asked.

"What if there's a curse on the room? I don't want to tempt the fates either."

"Pussy. I'll bring Marge, she'll bust that door down."

*

Chapter 7

Doyle drove back to the office and parked. They went in the back door and found Oscar at his desk.

"Did you catch your cheating spouse already?" Doyle asked in passing to his own desk.

"I followed him and he went into a motel room with his loose woman. She had to be a hooker. She didn't look very normal."

"What's normal?" Poppy asked him.

"She didn't look like the girl next door, or his secretary. I've rousted hookers many times on the force, so I know a hooker when I see one."

Poppy didn't debate him and she went to Marge's desk. "Did you read anything in your scandal magazine about ghosts haunting hotels in Detroit?"

Marge looked surprised and said, "Well, there were two. The Algonquin and the Regal. Both had great stories about hauntings. What do you need to know?"

"The Algonquin. We were just there and we heard some really interesting stories."

"The woman who hung herself in the death room?" Marge asked.

Poppy laughed and sat at her desk. "Talk to me about what you know."

"I only know what I read in the paper, Poppy. I don't really know much other than that. You could check the Detroit Public Library for more information. I'm sure they have the archives of the newspapers of that day."

"Marge, you have the computer in front of you that contains all the knowledge in the world. Couldn't we just look it up?" Poppy asked.

"Oh, right. Well, let's see what we can find." Marge turned to the computer and hit a few keys. "There we go. Jane Frobush, the woman who haunts the Algonquin. Shall I print out the page?"

"Sure, can you do that?" Poppy asked.

"I can do anything, I'm a super secretary," Marge snickered.

Doyle laughed at his desk. "Yes, Marge, you are a super secretary. I'll get you a cape to go with your costume."

"Halloween is coming up, I could use that costume," Marge answered.

"That's right, Marge. Halloween is coming up," Doyle said. "Strange, Poppy is on a case that involves a ghost and that goes with Halloween. Well timed, I'd say."

"I can do without the ghost. Halloween is fun, I can put up with that," Poppy said. "But I want to know more about this Frobush woman and what happened back then."

"That was before you were born," Doyle observed.

"A lot of things happened before I was born. You happened before I was born," Poppy replied.

"Not by much. I was ten when you were born."

"Such an older man. I need to find a younger man who can keep up with me," she smiled.

"I keep up with you just fine. Now read about your ghost so when we meet her, you two can have a nice talk," he said.

"Are you going to track down the Algonquin ghost?" Oscar asked. "I used to hear about the complaints filed on her. Guests at that hotel would call for police when they saw her. The cops never found the ghost, so they weren't happy when dispatch would send them to the hotel."

"Sounds like there's something to the stories, if that many people have seen her," Doyle finally admitted.

"So, now you believe that she exists?" Poppy asked.

"I didn't say that. I mean that I believe people saw something. It was a ghost or someone having fun with the guests by playing a ghost."

"Now why would someone go to the trouble of doing this every month for years? What do they have to gain?"

"I guess we have to capture the ghost to find out," Doyle replied just as Poppy's cell phone buzzed. She answered and listened, then hung up.

"That was my boss. He said Hallsey called him and said they had someone coming out the day after tomorrow to open the door. Since my boss now knows about the door, we can't go busting in."

"Why didn't Hallsey call you instead of your boss?" Doyle asked.

"I forgot to give him my card. Stupid thing to do. I didn't need him calling my company to say I wasn't doing my job. It's bad enough I put up with the other idiot investigators, without bringing my boss into this."

"You could quit the company and come work here. You have the experience and license to be a private investigator. Think about it," Doyle offered.

"Sure, and what if we broke up and hated each other? That would make for a hostile work environment."

Doyle thought about that. The way his luck was going with women, it could very well happen. Hard to work with an ex-girlfriend.

Marge spoke up, "You two could get married. That may solve that problem."

Doyle and Poppy both gave Marge a stare. Doyle spoke first. "I think that's for when she and I get to know each other better. We've only been seeing each other for a couple months."

"Definitely not long enough to get to know Doyle," Poppy said to Marge. "He's an enigma, and he's not easy to read."

"I like to be mysterious," Doyle said with a grin.

"Oh, Arthur, you're a nice guy and I can read you like a book," Marge said.

Doyle's Haunting

"Yes, a mystery book with the last few pages missing," Poppy added.

"I'm unfinished. More to be written about my exciting life," Doyle said with a wry smile. "Oscar, you've known me for a while. Do you think I'm mysterious?"

Oscar looked up from his paperwork and said, "I think you have a way about you that people can't put their finger on. As for mysterious, I don't think you're the type. You tend to bull your way through cases. Take no prisoners and damn the torpedoes, full speed ahead. That kind of guy."

"Thank you for that, Oscar. Very well said. I like to get to the heart of the matter, at all costs," Doyle said.

"That's what makes you a good investigator, Arthur," Marge said.

"Well, we'll see how good he is if he can find the ghost," Poppy threw in.

"I thought this was your case. When did I get hired to help? Are you paying me for my investigative time?"

"I'll reimburse you later," Poppy said with a wink. "Let's just find the ghost first."

"We have to wait until the day after tomorrow, remember. I think we need to go up and see my new cabin until then. Are you game for a road trip?" he asked her.

"Your new cabin?" Marge asked. "Is it ready for you to move in?"

"I don't know. Poppy said it was ready, according to the contractor. So we should go up and see what needs to be done."

"Yeah, getting out of the city sounds good right now." Poppy said. "I'll call work and make an excuse about checking the building, and whether the contractor did a good job bringing it in under cost."

"So call and we can go for a ride," Doyle said.

Doyle looked at Oscar. "You have command now, take care of Marge."

Oscar grinned. "I'll make sure the office doesn't go to hell. You go have fun with the wild life up there."

Poppy stood and said, "I'll call later, let's go. I want to see the autumn colors before the leaves fall off the trees."

*

Chapter 8

Doyle drove back to his apartment to grab his overnight bag that he kept packed in case of quick getaways. Poppy followed him in her car to leave it there.

About a half hour later and one call to Poppy's office, they were on their way to the cabin near the Metamora State Park campground. They got on I-75 and headed north as Poppy was watching for the fall colors of the tree leaves. It was a beautiful time of the year. Unfortunately, that meant snow would be coming soon. In Michigan snow could sneak in anytime from around Halloween to New Years.

They got off the freeway and headed up through Oxford, where Doyle grew up and into the woods where Doyle's cabin was. Doyle had called his friend, Sheriff Mike Twain, to get the keys to the building from Mike's brother-in-law. He was the contractor who re-built the cabin. Doyle thought back on when he rushed out of his former cabin leaving his enemy, Skeeter, to disarm the bomb that he planted. Doyle knew Skeeter wouldn't be able to do the job, so the cabin, along with Skeeter blew to smithereens.

Bob Moats

Doyle pulled into the long dirt drive to the cabin and saw a sheriff's car parked in front. He parked next to it and they got out. Poppy stretched as Doyle went to the cabin to see where his friend Mike was. Mike was on the new porch sitting in one of the wooden lawn chairs that survived the blast.

"Do you have a beer open for me?" Doyle said with a laugh.

"You can get your own beer," Mike said as Doyle surveyed the front of the cabin. It was more modern than the log style of the former cabin. He looked closer and found it was aluminum siding.

"Well, it looks great," he said as Poppy came around to them. "You remember my insurance investigator?"

"I do. How are you Poppy? Still with this lunk-head?"

She laughed, "Yep, I'll keep him as long as he's useful."

"Well, have you gone in yet?" Doyle asked his friend.

"Nope, I was waiting for you. I have been inside while my brother-in-law was building it. It's set up real nice. I think you'll like it," Mike said as he stood and handed the keys to Doyle.

Doyle's Haunting

Doyle handed the keys to Poppy and said, "Do me the honors."

She went to the door and unlocked it. She swung the door open and went in. The men followed her into the empty room.

"I see I'll need to get some furniture. Mike, do you have a brother-in-law who sells furniture?"

"No, but I have a cousin in the business, though," Mike said with a grin.

"We'll have to go visit him. I need furniture," he said and looked at Poppy. "Shall we go play house and furnish this thing?"

"I'm game," Poppy said as she checked the bathroom. "Nice and big, with a bathtub and shower. Sweet."

Doyle looked at Mike. "She's big into bathtubs."

"I like to soak every now and then, yes," she replied.

Mike's radio squawked, so he pulled the microphone and answered. They were calling him to an accident on Baldwin Road.

"Sorry, guys, duty calls. Go to Larry's Fine Furniture and tell him I sent you. He won't overcharge you by much."

"Thanks," Doyle said as Mike left them. Doyle checked out the bedroom and the kitchen. "This seems more like a house than a cabin. It's nice though, I could get used to it."

"Thinking of moving out here one day?" Poppy asked.

"I've always said when I retire I'll stay out here. The city is nice, but I grew up in the country life. I'll go back to it and the quiet."

"Well, you can't move in until you have furniture. Shall we go find Larry?"

Doyle took her back to his car and they drove over to Baldwin Road, where most stores were located. After a little driving they found the store. They went in and were greeted by an overly friendly salesperson.

"We're looking for Larry, are you him?" Doyle asked.

"No, I'll get him," he said and disappeared to the back.

Doyle's Haunting

Poppy was walking around the couches checking them out. "We should get one that pulls out into a bed. Just in case Oscar comes to visit."

"Just make sure it's not too comfortable, or he'll never leave," Doyle joked.

"Hello, may I help you?' Larry said, coming over. "Say, aren't you Art Doyle? I remember you from school," the man gave a big smile and held out his hand to shake. Doyle obliged him.

"I am Art Doyle. I guess I haven't changed that much since back then."

"Good to see you again. What can I do for you today?"

"I have a cabin that was rebuilt and need to furnish it," Doyle replied.

"Is that the one over on Lake Metamora that was blown up?" he asked. "I heard about that. That was your cabin?"

"It was, and your cousin, Mike Twain, had his brother-in-law rebuild it. Now I need furniture."

"You came to the right place and I'll give you a family discount. Let's go shopping."

Doyle thought he was too anxious, but allowed for it, just to get the furniture. They wandered as Poppy picked out different chairs and tables. Doyle just followed her and grinned. "Can you deliver this all tomorrow? We're only up here until tomorrow night."

"I'll have it all on the truck today and out early in the morning. I guarantee it or it's free," he said.

"Be careful saying that. Your truck could break down," Doyle warned.

Larry thought about that. "You're right. I'll try my best to get it to you by morning."

"That's better, now I need to find an Army surplus store. Do you know one?" Doyle asked.

Larry gave them directions and Doyle gave the man his credit card. The sale was finalized and they shook on it. Doyle and Poppy left the store and went back to the car.

"Army surplus store? Why?" Poppy asked.

"We'll need an air mattress to sleep on tonight and some blankets. We can sit outside on the lawn chairs while you fish."

"I didn't bring my fishing gear," she said

Doyle's Haunting

"Well, I'm sure the worms will thank you for that."

"Just find me a piece of string and a safety pin and I can catch us dinner," she laughed.

"I'm sure the Army surplus store will have what you need to fish. Shall we go?"

They drove to where Larry directed them and found the store. They went in and found a very old looking man at the counter. They greeted him and looked around for supplies for the night. Poppy laughed when she found a junior fisherman kit with plastic rod and reel. They gathered the supplies and went to pay.

"Howdy, did you find everything you need?" the elderly man asked.

"We did, thank you," Poppy replied.

The man lifted the fishing kit and said, "Your youngsters will enjoy this."

"We don't have any youngsters," Doyle said.

"Oh, yes, you two are a bit old for having youngsters," he smiled.

"The fishing kit is for me," Poppy said. "Do I need a license to fish?"

The man smiled and said, "You sure do. I can get you set up with that."

Doyle smiled and said, "Do you carry worms?"

*

Chapter 9

Supplies for the night were loaded into the car and they drove back to the cabin. As Doyle pulled into the long drive, he could see the sheriff's car by the cabin.

"I wonder why Mike is back?" he asked. They parked as Mike came around the cabin and went up to them.

"Mike, what's up? Did you miss us?" Doyle asked.

"I have a question and a small problem. The city is setting up a haunted house for Halloween, and now people are saying there's a demon in the place. Do you think you can look into it?"

"What the hell? Is this spook week for us?" he asked Poppy, then turned to Mike. "What kind of demon?"

"Well, the building is old and hasn't been used for a while. My brother-in-law was asked to make sure the building was safe for trick or treaters and he started to work on the maze that people would go through to be frightened. Now he won't go back in because he heard growls that were not from any animal that he knew. He said he saw glowing eyes in the basement and heard a snarling. He said he was done and hoped no one would be harmed. You don't believe in spirits, other than alcohol, so maybe you and Poppy could investigate the demon."

"Why don't you go in and see what it is?" Doyle asked.

"No thanks, I'm not going to be eaten by some demon dog," Mike said.

"Oh, so it's alright for us to go in and be eaten?" Doyle asked.

"Sure, you don't live here now, you just visit every so often, so people won't miss you."

"Where is this house?" Doyle inquired as he unloaded the car.

"Okay, that's another problem. It's Skeeter's old house." Mike moved back waiting for Doyle to explode.

"What?" Doyle yelled. "Are you crazy? That house held dead people and bodies were buried in the backyard. It's filled with Skeeter's evil spirit and you want to send little children through it? That man blew up my cabin. Are you going to tell people the back story of the house before you send them in to their deaths?"

"It wasn't my idea. I protested it. But the city council thought it would be appropriate for Halloween," Mike said.

"Appropriate? Why don't you tell the city council to stay one night in that house and see if it's appropriate?" Doyle took the packages to the cabin, followed by Poppy who had an arm full of things. Mike followed them.

"How are they going to advertise it?" Doyle asked. "I can see it now, 'Visit the haunted house formerly owned by a serial killer. Enjoy the real blood on the walls of the basement. Look for new shallow graves in the back yard. Find a real dead body and win a prize.' Is that how it's going to go?"

Doyle's Haunting

"Art, I just need you to take a look and see if you can figure out what's going on?" Mike asked.

Doyle stood looking at his friend. "Okay, if I get eaten by a demon, I'm haunting you for the rest of your miserable life." He looked at Poppy. "Are you up for this?"

"I'm game if Mike goes in with us. Along with all his deputies."

Doyle laughed and asked Mike, "Is that good for you?"

"I can probably convince one or two of them into going with us. When can you go?"

"Not that I'm anxious to go back to Skeeter's house, but whenever you say. Right now? Is that good for you?"

"I can handle that. Do you remember where the house is?" Mike asked.

"Mike, I couldn't forget it. I'll see you there shortly after we put our stuff in the cabin."

"Okay, I'll be there." He left them.

"I wasn't around when you had Skeeter causing you problems. Was he that bad?"

"Poppy, sit in the lawn chair and I'll tell you a real scary story." She sat and Doyle explained the whole sordid affair. She was amazed by all the murders and Skeeter getting away with it.

"So he was blown up in the old cabin on this property." Doyle explained. "They couldn't even find anything left of him. He was right on top of the bomb when it vaporized his body. That's what the ME said. I would have preferred that some body parts were left, so we could bury him in a shallow grave like he did to the poor women he murdered."

"Well, that is scary. So Skeeter's ashes could still be here in the grass?"

"You could look at it that way. I hope they vacuumed the grounds for him along with the ashes from the cabin."

"Shall we go find the demon haunting his house?" she asked.

"I've been stalling, but may as well go get it over with."

They left the cabin and Doyle drove to the house. He could see Mike's car and one other sheriff's car parked in the front. He parked on the grass next to the cars. They got out and found Mike at the side door.

Doyle's Haunting

"Thanks for coming, Art. There's something going on in here and we need to find out what's up. I don't believe in ghosts or demons, so let's clean this up."

"Do you think someone is trying to keep people away from this house?" Poppy asked. "By scaring people away?"

"Could be. It seems strange that there's a demon now, just after we went into the house," Mike said. "No one ever reported ghosts in the house. Although no one ever goes in the house."

"Okay. Let's go into the bowels of hell," Doyle said.

Mike used a key to unlock the door and pushed it open. He waved Doyle to go in.

"Thanks, I get to go first?" Doyle asked. As he entered, he asked, "Was this place swept good for hidden rooms?"

"I don't know. After the forensic team from the State police went through the building they didn't say they found any strange rooms that I know. Why?"

"Well, if there is a demon or someone pretending to be a demon, then it has to have a hiding place."

"True, let's give it a good search," Mike said as they went down the stairs into the basement.

"Since it's still fairly light out, the demon shouldn't come out," Poppy said.

"I hope so. I've never seen a demon. If we find one, please don't stand behind me," Doyle said with a grin.

They moved around the basement, that was still a mess from Skeeter's debauchery of human sacrifice.

"Didn't your brother-in-law clean this place up?" Doyle asked seeing the blood still on the walls and floors.

"I presume he thought it was cute. I didn't know he left it," Mike said.

"Okay, we need to examine this basement for any hidden rooms. There has to be a hidden room for the demon to hide in." Doyle said.

The four of them scouted the three rooms in the basement, the laundry, and two storage rooms. One had been used to dissect humans. Poppy avoided that room. She went into the other storage room and searched the walls for doors to hidden rooms.

Doyle went into the room after her and found her missing. He felt a chill and yelled for Mike. He came running into the room and asked, "What?"

"We have a problem," Doyle said.

*

Chapter 10

"What?" Mike asked, coming into the room.

"I followed Poppy into this room and now she's gone. Get your deputy in here to help tear this room apart," he yelled as he was beating on walls. Mike called for his man to come in to help search.

"If there's a hidden room, it has to be in here. Poppy just didn't vanish into thin air." The men kicked and beat on the walls until one wall sounded hollow. Doyle stood back checking the wall for seams or a panel of a door. The wall had shelves in front, but Doyle looked to the floor and saw scrape marks where the door had opened. He pulled on the shelves and they didn't move.

"Damn it, pull on this sucker," he yelled. The three men pulled on the shelves and then it gave way. The shelves moved from the wall but the wall didn't open. Doyle could see where the seam for the door was now and he looked around the room for something to pry it open.

Mike told his deputy to go get a crowbar from the car. He ran off and then shortly after, came in with a huge crowbar.

"Who would be back there?" Mike asked.

"Skeeter had a few friends that helped him in his crimes. They probably are holed up here." Doyle took the big crowbar and rammed it into the seam of the door. He pushed on the bar and then Mike and the deputy helped. They strained to pry the door open and finally they felt it give way a little. Doyle could see where there was a lock on the other side and pulled his Sig and started firing at the lock.

Finally the door gave way and opened. Doyle had his Sig up and was waiting for gunfire. There was none. They rushed in and found a man holding Poppy in a choke hold, with a gun to her head.

The man showed scars of being badly burned all over his head and hands. Doyle suddenly realized who he was. "Damn it, Skeeter, you just wouldn't die, would you?"

Doyle's Haunting

"Screw you, Doyle, I had a good thing going until you stuck your nose in it."

"You were the one dumping bodies on my property and following me around. So don't blame me for your stupidity."

"Brave words when I have the life of this woman in my hands," he said sneering. His face was so burned away, he was a melted image of his former self.

"Skeeter, how did you get away from the explosion?" Doyle asked stalling for time.

He laughed and said. "After you rushed out leaving me to die, I decided to cut that plastic cuff you put on me instead of defusing the bomb. I knew I couldn't do it, I made the bomb too well. I cut the cuff with my pocket knife and was running out the door just as the bomb blew. I was caught in the flames and ran to the lake to extinguish myself but I was still badly burned, as you can see. I'm surprised you recognized me."

"I can see the evil in you, Skeeter, burned or not," Doyle said.

"Stop calling me Skeeter!" he screamed. "My name is Bill. Call me Bill or I'll blow her brains out."

"Come on, Skeeter, you know you're trapped. If you kill her, I'll kill you. So you can give up and go to prison for the crimes you committed or die. I don't think you want to die or you wouldn't have come back here to hide."

"I'm not going to prison, so I guess we have a standoff," he screamed.

Doyle tensed up. It was close as to whether Skeeter would shoot Poppy and die, or give up. Doyle didn't think he would give up that easily. He looked at Poppy and she smiled.

"You can give me a nice scar if you want," she said referring to the shot that gave the Mayor of Detroit a scar on the side of his face when Doyle shot Crazy Joe in the head.

Doyle grinned, "I've been practicing," he said and aimed for Skeeter's head. "Last chance, Bill," he said and pulled the trigger. "Oops, too late to decide," he spoke, quietly to himself.

Skeeter's head snapped back and he went down. Poppy ran to Doyle and grabbed on to him. Mike and the deputy went to Skeeter to check him.

"He's definitely dead this time," Mike said.

Doyle's Haunting

"Good, put him in a shallow grave out in the woods and don't mark it," Doyle growled as he held a shaking Poppy.

An hour later, the county coroner was out to take the body and everyone was sitting on the front porch.

"My God, that was the monster who gave you the hard time months ago?" Poppy asked. "I feel so violated."

"Not as violated as what I'll do to you later in the cabin," Doyle laughed.

Doyle turned to Mike and said, "I think we cleared the demon problem. I'll send you the bill for services soon."

"Why did Skeeter come back here?" Mike asked.

"He had a safe place with the hidden room to go to until your city council decided to get close to his hiding place. He did his best to frighten away your brother-in-law and may have succeeded if I hadn't been up here."

He looked at Poppy and said, "Are you all right now?"

She replied, "I'm still a little shaken by this. He came out of that hidden room so quietly and grabbed me from behind. I didn't even see him."

The deputy came around the house and said, "He had a nice setup down there. It was a survival room with food and supplies to live nicely for a long time."

"I'm sure he was plotting to get back at you one day. Luckily you were in the neighborhood to stop him," Mike said.

Doyle smiled and said, "I almost feel sorry for him."

"Why in the world would you do that?" Poppy asked, incredulously.

"He was a miserable person. No one liked him and he survived the explosion only to end up here to hide, alone. Now he's been put out of his misery before he could do his plotting. Sad ending to a sad man."

"You make him out to be a victim, he's not. He murdered people you knew and killed all those women. Don't lose sleep over his death. He died in the explosion, so leave him there."

Doyle smiled and kissed her on the cheek. "You can be mean when you want to be, whether it's with humans or worms."

Doyle's Haunting

"Speaking of worms, I need to go fishing," she said. "Let's get away from this place and back to the cabin."

Doyle sighed and stood. He helped her up and turned to Mike. "Thanks for the adventure. I'm getting my fill of Halloween treats. We still have to go back and chase a ghost in a hotel in Detroit. Don't tell me what you do with Skeeter's body. I'm not interested."

"Thanks for the help, Art. It's something to tell the city council about," Mike replied.

"Yeah, hope their haunted house is a success. Talk later. I got fish to clean and cook."

He grinned and took Poppy to the car.

*

Chapter 11

Poppy managed to catch a couple of lake bass of which she was very proud. They were small but edible. "I could very easily live up here. This is nice," she said.

"I've had this property for years and always came up here to recharge my mind. It has that effect. I got the air mattress set up but we don't have anything to fry the fish on, the new stove won't get here until tomorrow morning."

"You have a fire pit in the yard. We can put the fish on sticks and cook them that way."

"You'd be handy if we were lost in the woods somewhere," he said with a laugh. "I did pick up a plastic dinner set at the store. So we can eat off plates at least. I don't want to be a savage and eat from a stick."

She laughed and they took the fish to the cabin. Poppy said she'd like to fix the fire, so she went off to collect wood from the fallen trees behind the cabin. Doyle said he was going to call Oscar and tell him about Skeeter.

Doyle's Haunting

He sat on a lawn chair and dialed Oscar's number.

"How's the new cabin?" Oscar asked when he answered.

"Great, but you're going to love what I have to tell you." He gave Oscar the details of his afternoon chasing a demon.

"Damn, I wish I had been there. I can't believe Skeeter survived the blast," Oscar said.

"Total surprise to me. Although, I never did like the coroner's explanation of why there was nothing left of Skeeter's body in the wreckage. I guess I expected him to show back up one day. Now I know he's really dead and gone. Only his ghost could come back now," Doyle said with a laugh.

"Everything here is fine. Marge is becoming obsessed reading up on that ghost you and Poppy are chasing. The internet really has lots of information on just about everything. I have another spousal infidelity case to take care of, so she can spend the rest of tomorrow reading."

"Good to hear that all is well. I'll be back the morning after tomorrow to get ready to hunt the ghost. Keep cool," he said and they finished the call.

Poppy was trying to start the fire in the pit as Doyle came over to her. "I have some paper in the car to help start it," he said.

"That would help," she replied.

He went to get the paper and returned with it to give her. She tore a couple pages and stuck them under the wood. A few minutes later the fire was building up nicely.

"We don't have a side dish to go with the fish," she said.

"You cook and I'll run to the little store one road over and get something." He left her and went to his car. He drove over to Baldwin Road and pulled into the small grocery store and parked in front. He went in and over to the small deli counter. He was checking the bowls of prepared foods when someone put hands over his eyes. He was ready to attack when he heard a female voice say, "Guess who?"

It was Amber, Doyle's last female conquest who decided he had too many criminals chasing him and taking her prisoner. He stood up and turned to her. She gave him a big kiss on the lips. He was glad he hadn't brought Poppy or she might have been offended.

Doyle's Haunting

He moved her back gently and said, "Amber, good to see you. Now that you're here, I have some news to tell you. Skeeter is dead."

"I know. I was there when he blew up your cabin," she replied.

"No, it turns out he didn't die. He survived and was hiding out in his house here in town. About two hours ago, I shot him and he's now officially dead."

"Oh, God. He was still around the area. That frightens me."

"Well, he's gone now, so relax. How are you? Still working at the bar?"

"I am. Are you still single and free to dance?"

"Uh, no. I have a new girlfriend and she's in the same business as I am. She's an investigator for an insurance company."

"So the two of you can chase criminals together?" she said with a coy smile.

"I guess you could say that. We get along well."

"You'll have to bring her to the bar so I can approve her."

"I don't know about that, Amber. The two of you will just sit around talking about me. I don't think I can handle that. If you promise to not talk about our relationship, I may bring her."

"Are you ashamed of me?" she said indignantly.

"No, I just don't need an ex-girlfriend and a new girlfriend comparing notes. That's all."

Amber laughed and smiled. "Art, you were a great lover and I wouldn't embarrass you by talking about you like that to your new love. Besides, I have a boyfriend of my own now."

"Well, I'm really glad for you. I hope he's not in law enforcement. You don't need that again."

No, he's a doctor. A nice, safe man. He heals people while you shoot people." She laughed again. "I met him through friends. We've been dating for about a month now."

"Okay, you bring him to the bar and I'll bring my girlfriend and we'll sit around talking about our prowess in bed."

"Never mind, I'll take your word that your new girlfriend is nice. Glad she's a copy of you for crime fighting. That's the kind of woman you need. Also glad to hear Skeeter is really dead now. I wondered when they didn't find anything left of him in the remains of your cabin."

"I have to go, there's fish cooking over a fire and I need a side dish."

"She got you domesticated?"

"I think so sometimes. Good to see you again."

"Don't stay a stranger. We shared some good times along with the bad." She kissed his cheek and went off. Doyle watched her walk away, admiring her great hind end. It was what attracted him to her when they first met. He had to get Poppy's great body into his head, so he turned back to the food and ordered some potato salad. He left the store and drove back to the cabin, thinking about his time up here with Amber and Skeeter. Good and bad, it was now a memory.

He pulled into the drive and parked. Poppy was still cooking the fish over the fire and he handed her the bag with the potato salad. He had another larger bag and set that on the porch.

She looked into the bag he gave her and said, "Good choice, I like potato salad. It will go nicely with the fish. What's in the other bag?"

Doyle smiled and said, "Something to chase down the food."

"Beer, I suppose."

"Yep. Now is the fish ready to eat?" Doyle asked looking at the fish smoking on the sticks.

"Go get the plates and we can eat outside."

They ate and were happy with the way the fish came out, although Doyle wasn't crazy about eating a fish with the head still on. "I'm not crazy about a fish watching me while I eat him."

"I hope you cut the head and tail off before you ate it."

"Of course, I'm not a savage," he laughed.

*

Chapter 12

They sat watching the fire die down. Doyle had gathered some more wood to burn, but it was getting late now, and Poppy was nodding off. Doyle scattered the last of the burning embers in the fire pit to die out and helped Poppy up. They went in the cabin and Poppy headed straight for the bedroom, dropping her clothes, and crawled on the air mattress.

Doyle looked around the empty living room and imagined what the new furniture would be like. They had stopped at an appliance store and ordered a refrigerator and stove. They promised to deliver tomorrow, also. It was going to be a busy day moving furniture around and making the cabin livable.

He was happy with his life now. His business was going well and he had a little extra money in the bank to get him and his agency through any problems. His cabin was new now and the furniture would be a welcome relief. The woman in his bedroom was becoming more of a part of his life and she made him happy. He had no regrets now and even relaxed knowing that Skeeter was really dead. It had always bothered him not knowing.

He went to the bedroom and could hear Poppy breathing softly as she slept. He undressed and crawled under the covers. He slept well that first night in his new cabin.

~~*~~

There was a banging on the cabin door very early the next morning. Doyle grumbled a few obscenities and crawled out of bed, pulling on his pants. He went into the living room, looked through the front window and saw a number of boxes on the front porch. It was the furniture company. Doyle looked at his watch and it was just before seven.

"Too damn early to make deliveries," he mumbled. Poppy came out of the bedroom, dressed. Doyle opened the door and found Larry standing there.

"You own the company, sell stuff and deliver. It must save you on employees," Doyle said trying to wake up.

"I came out personally after talking to my cousin, Mike. He told me about your adventures yesterday. I must say I was impressed. I've never meet a real P.I. so you are my first. We have your furniture to put in your cabin, may we come in?"

"So, do your thing. I'm going to sit on the porch and watch," he said and went to sit down.

Doyle's Haunting

Larry proceeded to tell his men to take the furniture in as Poppy directed their movements. Doyle figured she would arrange the furnishings and then later he could rearrange everything to his liking. Not that he didn't think Poppy could do a good job, but he was particular about how he wanted everything to be set up.

Forty minutes later, they had finished and were packing the empty boxes back in the truck. Larry came back over to Doyle and smiled.

"I hope you enjoy the furniture. I'm glad to have served you." He nodded to Poppy and went off to the truck.

"Now all we need is the refrigerator and the stove," Poppy said as Larry and his crew drove off.

Doyle stood and went in the cabin and was pleased with Poppy's arrangements. "Looks good, babe. You did a good job," he said and kissed her.

They relaxed on the couch and watched the TV on the new entertainment center. Shortly after, the appliances arrived and were put in place. As they stood looking at the shiny new fridge and stove, Doyle said, "Now we need some food, but not a lot since we won't be up here that often."

"Frozen pizza will keep," she said with a grin.

"Yeah, I guess we can get some frozen foods. They'll keep."

They went to the small grocery store where Doyle ran into Amber. He hoped she didn't pop up again. They bought canned goods and frozen foods and took them back to the cabin.

Again, they relaxed on the couch.

"What do you think we'll find in the locked room tomorrow?" Poppy asked.

"I hope no dead bodies. I don't think I need to see any more after dealing with Skeeter and then the ones on the island."

"The more I think about my ghost sighting, I may have been dreaming. I was in bed at the time, so I could have been asleep. But it seemed so real."

"I'm sure you saw something." Doyle said. "Dream or otherwise, you remembered it. I'm sure the ghost in the hotel has a good reason for hanging around."

"Since it's been seen for a number of years, I have to believe that it's something. Too long for one person to pretend to be haunting the hotel. Besides, no one there, other than the old man in the wheelchair down in the basement, has been around long enough to do this. So why couldn't it be a ghost? Look at all the most famous haunted house and castles, what's their explanation? "

"There are more things in heaven and earth than dreamt of in your mind, Horatio." Doyle said.

"Nice try. It's 'There are more things in heaven and earth, Horatio, than are dreamt of in your philosophy.' But you were close. Yes, there are lots of unexplained things going on around us. Ones we can't explain."

"Aliens," Doyle said.

"What?"

"Aliens are behind it all."

"You don't believe in ghosts, but you believe in aliens."

"Of course. I've seen flying saucers, so they must be real," Doyle said with a grin.

"When did you see a flying saucer?" Poppy asked pointedly.

"I was on assignment with the FBI to track some bad guys in the foothills of Montana, and it was late at night when these lights flew overhead and hovered for a few minutes then shot up into space. Had to be aliens."

"Swamp gas," Poppy laughed.

"There were no swamps near the foothills. That was an explanation years ago by the government to dispel sightings, like weather balloons."

"Okay, so you saw a flying saucer and I saw a ghost. Neither of us has any way of proving what we saw. We just have to believe ourselves."

"That works for me," Doyle said, "although there were six other men I was with when we saw the saucer. So I have witnesses, what do you have?"

She thought for a moment and then said, "My teddy bear. It was with me when I saw the ghost."

"So, I can't produce the six other guys and you can't produce your teddy. I guess it's just our word on it."

"I'll agree to that," Poppy said with a laugh. "Now, I'm tired and we have a long drive in the morning. Let's get some sleep."

She stood and headed to the new bed as Doyle sat there. He was thinking about the locked door and what could be behind it. They were told about the serial killer hiding in there. Could he have seen the ghost? If he had, why would he hide up there? And why didn't anyone know he was up there? That attic must hold the key to something and he wanted to find it.

Poppy yelled from the bedroom, "Are you coming to bed? I'm naked on our new mattress."

Doyle didn't think twice.

*

Chapter 13

Early next morning, they tested the shower and it worked fine. They toweled off and dressed, then got the cabin ready to be vacant for a while. The drive down to Detroit was quick and quiet. They both were lost in their thoughts about the mystery room and what it could contain.

"This could be another Al Capone's safe like when Geraldo Rivera opened the thing and it was empty." Poppy said.

"Well, we know something is in the room because of the crashing noise and the fact we heard a cat. It had to have an opening to get in the room," Doyle said.

"Maybe the old lady ghost is a cat lady with fifteen cats. I hate to see that room, if she doesn't go out for kitty litter," Poppy laughed and relaxed.

Doyle drove into his apartment parking lot and pulled next to Poppy's car. "Are you going to follow me to the office?"

"I'm running by my apartment first to change clothes. I really should have an overnight bag like you do. I'll see you shortly." She kissed him and went out to her car.

Doyle went into his apartment to quickly check that everything was good and listen to his answering machine. He had no messages, so he went out to go to the office. He arrived and found Oscar's car was not there, hopefully he was on a case. He went in and Marge was staring at her computer.

"What's so interesting, Marge?" Doyle asked.

"I was reading about your ghost. Seems she started haunting the hotel on the anniversary of her lover's death the next year."

Doyle's Haunting

"Since 1946? That's a long time to mourn for a man. He must have been special. What did she do when the hotel was closed down?"

"Well, there were a number of reports that kids broke into the hotel and were frightened half to death by the ghost. The police were called by the kids, but they never found anything."

"I'm amazed there were so many people seeing this ghost. I don't believe in them, but I'm outnumbered by the facts."

The back door opened and in came Poppy. She came up to Marge and Doyle and waited.

"Feel better?" Doyle asked, noting her new clothes.

"I do, and I called Hallsey and he said he has people coming to force the door. They plan on being there around noon. So if you want to go grab a bite to eat before then, let's move."

"You want fish?"

"Not really, but a breakfast sandwich would be nice."

"Breakfast sandwich?" he asked.

"It's egg, sausage, and cheese on a bun. They're good."

"Okay let's go," he said. "Marge, we'll be back shortly. If you can find out anything more on our ghost, I'd appreciate it."

They left and went to Burger King for the breakfast sandwich. Doyle had to admit it was good. They drove back and found Oscar's car was now in.

"Oscar, what case are you on now?" Doyle asked as they came in.

"What do you think? Cheating wife, of course." Oscar was looking unhappy, Doyle could see this.

"How would you like to go with Poppy and me to chase a ghost?"

Oscar perked up and said, "I'd like that. When?"

Doyle looked at his watch and said, "Now, if you have nothing else to do?"

"Hey, a chance to see a ghost. I'm ready to go," Oscar said with a smile.

They all went out to Doyle's car and he drove back to the hotel. They went into the lobby where they found Mr. Hallsey standing by the front desk. He didn't smile as they came up.

Doyle's Haunting

"You look upset? Now what?" Doyle asked him.

"The company was not happy about the room being broken into, but I explained the problem with the insurance. They yielded. There should be some men from a construction company coming in shortly to open the door."

"Good, we'll be up there waiting," Doyle said. They started for the stairs, but Doyle stopped and asked, "Are there any guests staying on that floor?"

"No, not at the moment. This week is the full moon and we don't like putting people up there."

"Okay, we'll be waiting." Doyle, Poppy and Oscar climbed the stairs and ended up on the fifth floor.

"Damn, couldn't we have taken the elevator?" Oscar asked.

"Oscar, you need the exercise," Doyle said.

"No, I don't. I'm taking the elevator back down when we're done," Oscar said.

Doyle pointed to the wire cage and said, "Be my guest."

Oscar went to the elevator and looked down. "This thing has to be a century old. I'm not riding in it. Going down is easier than coming up stairs."

"Smart man," Doyle said and proceeded to pick the lock on the attic door again. Doyle said quietly to Poppy, "Let's let Oscar go in first."

"You are cruel," she said.

He opened the door and said to Oscar, "After you."

He thanked Doyle and went up the couple of short stairs into the attic. He got about ten feet in when he came up to the moose and screamed.

Doyle and Poppy both laughed. "You knew that was up here didn't you?" he said, turning back to them. "That was mean."

"It got your heart rate up, didn't it?" Doyle asked.

"So did climbing the stairs. Any more surprises to get my heart racing?"

"Just a ghost, if we disturb it by breaking down the door," Doyle replied.

"So, where's this door?" Oscar asked.

Doyle's Haunting

Doyle pointed to the back of the room, where the door stood defying them to get through.

Oscar went to it and felt around the frame. "It's of good workmanship. Solid frame and thick door," he said feeling the door at the bottom, sticking his fingers in the narrow crack. "Ow!" he yelled.

"What?" Doyle asked.

"Something bit me. Look, it drew blood." He held out his fingers showing the tiny trace of blood. "Geez, I hope I don't get some disease now. What if it's a rat bite, I could die."

Poppy reached into her purse and brought out a tissue for him. He cleaned the bite and held the tissue to his finger. "There's something in there and it ain't friendly," he said.

Doyle kicked the door again and they heard another crash. This time there was no cat crying.

"They better get here quickly to open this door," he said looking around for something to pry the door with. He saw nothing.

There was a noise at the attic entrance and Hallsey came in with three big men in construction work clothes.

"I see you can get into the attic all right. Yet, you can't get in that door," Hallsey said snottily.

"There's no lock to pick, Roderick," Doyle replied. "Are these the men who'll open this door?"

One man who seemed to be in charge came up and looked at the door. "This shouldn't be a problem. Harry, bring the pry bar," he said to one of his men. They took the pry bar and tried to get it in the crack between the door and the frame. It was a tight fit, so they had to pound it in.

They worked on it, but it wouldn't budge. "Damn, I've gotten in tougher safes than this. What the hell is it made from?" the leader asked.

"Ghost stuff," Poppy muttered.

*

Chapter 14

"Harry, bring up the buzz saw," the crew leader told one of his men. He went off and they waited.

"What's the buzz saw?" Poppy asked.

"You'll see. It's so cool, it cuts through anything," one of the construction men said. "We're going to cut the door in the center, opening up a hole and see what's locking the door. There has to be locks all around this door. Which is why it won't give way to our pry bar."

Doyle figured they wouldn't get in too soon. "I'm going to explore the outside of the building. Keep an eye on the door and phone me if they get in," he said to Poppy, and left the room. He went out of the attic and studied the layout of the rooms on the fifth floor. He went to a door right next to the attic. He used his lock picks on the door and entered. It was a nice room, clean and smelled good. He was sure guests would find the room pleasant, even though a ghost was next door. He was in room 503, next to the death room of 504. He wasn't going in there. He went to the window and looked out.

It was over the back parking lot, a long way down. He had climbed buildings higher than this, so it was no problem. He climbed out on the ledge and looked for something to grab on to help him up to the roof. He found a way up and took it. He walked along the edge of the sloped roof, being careful where he stepped. He went in the direction of where the mystery room would be and found the dirty skylights of the attic.

He looked down into one and could see Poppy and Oscar waiting for the saw. He turned his attention to the area where the mystery room would be and crawled over. He found a skylight that wasn't over the attic proper. He tried to look in but it was painted over. This annoyed him so he took his elbow and ran it into a small glass panel of the skylight. It broke and now he could look in.

There was a huge blast of air coming out of the broken window and he almost fell back. He grabbed on to the edge of the skylight and held on while he got his footing again. He slowly brought his head up to the broken window and looked in again carefully.

It was dark in the room, too dark. The light from the skylight didn't help to brighten up the room. He tried to focus his eyes in the lack of light and he was able to finally make out furniture although there didn't appear to be anyone in the room. He watched for movement and waited. He could hear the saw start up.

Doyle's Haunting

~~*~~

Poppy watched the men getting the saw running. One man took the circular saw to the center of the door to cut a hole. He carefully put the fast rotating blade against the door and was knocked on his butt. The blade made a scream against something in the door that prevented it from cutting through.

The crew leader went to the door, looked in the cut and could see metal. "Damn, it's not just wood. This damn thing is metal inside of wood. I think we need the diamond tipped saw." He turned to his man and told him to go get it. The man left the room.

"Who put this door here?" the man asked Hallsey, who was standing back from the men.

"I have no idea, it's been here for years. We had no reason to go in there so we ignored it. When they were reopening the hotel and remodeling, they had problems getting in there," Hallsey said.

"Well, we can blast the door, but it may damage more of the hotel, even if we control the blast."

"No, no, don't do that. I'm responsible for damages. Just do your best." He was sweating now. Poppy was enjoying this.

The man returned with the saw and they hooked it up. He was just getting ready to cut the door when they heard a knocking. It was coming from the door.

They shut off the saw and listened. The knocking stopped and they heard what sounded like locks being opened. It got quiet then the door slowly opened. Everyone stood back and waited.

The door opened more and Doyle stuck his head out. "Hey, anyone ready to come in?"

Poppy went up to him and slapped him on the forehead. "You frightened me. Not nice. What's in there?"

He opened the door wide and said, "Come on in and see." He stood back and let them pass.

"How did you get in?" Poppy asked as she passed him by. He pointed up to the skylight. It was open now.

"I had to jump, but luckily there was a couch to break my fall," he said.

"Couch? Why is there a couch in here?"

"Well, I looked around before they tried to bust in, and it looks like someone was living up here. Not a crazed serial killer, but a normal person judging by the furniture. I didn't find any bodies either," he said with a smile. "This place has all the comforts of an efficiency apartment. Since the door locks from the inside only, I don't know how the tenant got in and out."

"I think I know," Oscar said from a dark corner of the room, behind a short wall. "There's a service elevator here, small but big enough for four people."

They went to see it and Hallsey asked, "Where in the world does that go to?"

Doyle looked at him and said, "Down." He grinned at the man and said, "Did you know anyone was up here?"

"Of course not. I was aware that there was a history of this room, but after the police arrested the serial killer, they cleaned out the room. Who could be living up here?"

"Do you know the purpose of this room?" Poppy asked.

"I never knew and never asked. I didn't explore the building and the serial killer was before I started managing the hotel. I had just heard about it and wasn't a part of it."

"Well, someone was living up here. It sure wasn't a ghost," Doyle said checking out the small apartment size refrigerator. "There's food in here. Not a lot but enough to live on." He opened the microwave and looked inside. "Ghosts don't need microwaves, do they?"

Poppy went to him and said, "Of course not. I'm curious to know who lives up here."

"Shall we take a ride in the elevator to see where it leads to?" Oscar commented. "Maybe that'll give us some idea of what is going on up here."

Poppy went to the elevator followed by Doyle. "It looks safe enough. Not really that old looking," she said.

"Well, it had to have been put in when the building was constructed. Kind of hard to stick it in after the fact." the construction leader said, standing behind them. They turned, realizing he was still with them.

"So this thing could be ancient? Does that mean it's not safe?" Doyle asked.

They all jumped when the motor of the elevator started up and the car went down.

"Looks like we may get an answer," Doyle said.

*

Chapter 15

They stood waiting as the elevator was coming back up. The metal door opened, and they realized it was Herman, from the basement janitorial supply room.

"What the hell are you people doing in here?" he yelled from the elevator. He moved his wheelchair out into the room as everyone moved back.

"What the hell are we doing here? What the hell are you doing up here?" Hallsey yelled back.

"I live here, you dang fool. Have been for twelve years and was happy to be left alone. Now I suppose I'll be bombarded by all the staff," he moaned.

Poppy went to him. "Herman, why have you hidden up here all these years?"

He looked at her and smiled. "I like you, so I'll tell you. After they took that serial killer out of here, I got curious and came up through the elevator. It had been locked off in the basement, but I found the way to get by it. They had cleaned out this room and it was perfect for me."

"How did you fix it up, being in a wheelchair?" Poppy asked.

The old man chuckled and said, "I have a cousin who helped bring furniture and things up here from the basement to set up my living area. Plenty of old furniture in storage in the basement. He also brings me food every week so I don't starve. I haven't been out of the hotel in twelve years. I have everything here to keep me happy."

"What was this room used for before the serial killer moved in?" Doyle asked.

"Back twenty years ago, it was a little apartment for the building handyman and the original janitor, Chester Highland. He could go from the basement to this room in the service elevator, so they let him stay up here. He died of old age, but they didn't clean the room out, then the idiot serial killer moved in. Turns out he was Chester's nephew and knew about his uncle living up here. So he quietly moved in. He had that door built so no one could get in, but when the cops found out where he was, they waited until he came out of the door to go use a shower in one of the rooms. That's how they got in."

"Interesting. But why didn't you tell Hallsey you were up here?" Doyle asked.

Doyle's Haunting

"What, and have the idiot bothering me? No offense, Hallsey," he said to the manager.

Hallsey was going to speak, but didn't after Poppy gave him a look.

"Since you've been up here, have you seen the old woman ghost?" Doyle asked.

"Jane Frobush? Sure, I talk to her every full moon," the old man smiled as everyone just stared. "Oh, take a breath, I was kidding. I've heard the rumors, but have never seen her. I don't go out into the hotel, just from the basement to my room. So she haunts the fifth floor, it's not a place I've been to."

"Your room is about ninety feet from room 504, where Jane hung herself, and you've never heard anything up here?" Doyle asked.

"I didn't say I've never heard anything. I just never saw her. I may have heard a woman crying from out there somewhere," he said pointing to the attic. "As long as she didn't bother me, I didn't bother her. Poor woman."

Hallsey stepped forward and said, "Well, Herman, I can't have you living up here. It's not hotel policy."

Poppy got right up in Hallsey's face and pushed him back. She growled, "Listen to me carefully. If you do anything to move this man out, I'll bring in building inspectors to tear this place apart for violations that will make your employers very unhappy. Do you understand?"

Hallsey looked shocked and nodded his head repeatedly.

"Good, and you will keep this to yourself. Now I can let my company know that the room is no danger to the building. Luckily, you have a man up here watching the place for you." She turned back to Doyle. "Let's get everyone out of here and let Herman live in peace." She looked to the man and he gave her a wink.

Everyone left, but Doyle, Poppy and Oscar. She turned to Herman and said, "Winfield said a ghost knocked her down the stairs. Do you believe her?"

"Hell, no. Look, she fell from the fourth floor stairs, the ghost never goes off the fifth floor, or so they say. Plus there was no full moon, so no ghost."

Poppy smiled and thanked him. She took out her card and handed it to him. "You ever need anything, you call me."

"Dinner and a little wine," he said with a grin.

"Hey, she's my girlfriend. I'll find you a woman," Doyle said, trying not to smile.

Doyle's Haunting

"Blond and well-built," he replied.

"I'll see what I can do. No promises."

"We'll leave you to your solitude. Sorry to intrude. By the way, how did you know we were up here?" Poppy asked.

"Motion sensors. They set off an alarm in my room downstairs," he replied pointing to a box in the corner of the room by the ceiling.

"Smart," she said and motioned to Doyle to leave.

Doyle paused. "We heard a cat up here earlier."

"Oh, that's Melville, he goes in and out through a hole in the wall that leads to the roof. He visits me often. He's a black cat, by the way," he said with a grin and a wink.

Doyle looked up and said, "I'll have someone come up and fix the broken pane in the skylight."

"No, I don't want anyone else up here." Herman said. "I'll have my cousin cover it over, but thanks for the offer."

Doyle nodded and turned to Poppy. "Shall we go?"

They went into the attic and closed the heavy door behind them and could hear the locks being put back in place.

"I guess that satisfies my curiosity about the mysterious room," Poppy said. "Now we still have to find our ghost."

"There is a full moon this week, shall we come and camp out?" Doyle asked.

"You do know Halloween is this week?" Poppy replied.

"Yes, I do, and how appropriate is that?" Doyle said. "Maybe the ghost will bring some friends to trick or treat?"

"Shall we call the Ghostbusters?" Oscar said.

"Who ya gonna call?" Doyle laughed.

They went back down to the lobby and found Hallsey standing at the front desk. They came up behind him and Poppy called his name. He jumped and turned.

"Ms. Drake, you startled me. I hope that satisfies you about the room?"

Doyle's Haunting

"I'll make my report, so you should be all right now. I still have to investigate the accident of Mrs. Winfield. May I ask why she was staying in the hotel in the first place, is she from out of town?"

"Yes, she comes into the city once every couple months to visit with relatives. She lives in Chicago."

"Has she reported seeing a ghost before?" Poppy asked.

"No, this was the first time."

"Mr. Doyle and I will be back on the full moon to see if we can see the ghost. We may need a room on that floor," Poppy requested.

"Just not 504," Doyle added, with a grin.

"Of course. Normally, we don't let guests stay on that floor during a full moon, too many problems. But you can have any room you want. I'll arrange it when you come back."

"Thank you, I'll be in touch," she said and led Doyle out.

Back in the car, Doyle said, "Well, that was interesting. Herman has a nice set-up going for him."

"He does, I hope they don't bother him, now that they know he's up there."

"I love it when you get tough with people. You had Hallsey almost wetting his pants." Doyle said.

"Yes, I do enjoy that," she said with a sly smile.

*

Chapter 16

They arrived back at the office. Oscar went to his desk as Doyle and Poppy went to Marge's desk.

"So, what have you found out about Jane Frobush?" Doyle asked.

"Have a seat, I've got a few things to tell you." Poppy took the seat next to the desk and Doyle pulled a chair over and sat. "I did some digging and it seems that hotel has had its share of deaths."

"I remember Hallsey saying something about numerous deaths," Doyle said.

"The first was a woman murdered in her room by her husband. No mystery there, he confessed. But he said he was possessed by a spirit making him kill his wife. He blamed the ghost of Frobush for his actions. The jury didn't see it that way. He's still in prison."

"When did that happen?" Doyle asked.

"Eight years ago. Now another death that was unexplained happened four years ago. A man was found dead in the spa. They say he had a shocked look on his face. No bodily injuries or drugs in his system, so they listed it as heart failure. Maybe he saw a ghost," Marge said with a laugh. "There was one more death, a woman jumped from her fifth floor room to her death in the parking lot below."

"Fifth floor? Was there any mention of what room number?"

"The article didn't say, but the date of the death was something I checked on. I went to the sky charts and found that on that night there was a full moon."

Doyle looked at Poppy. "Hallsey said they don't put people on the fifth floor rooms during a full moon."

"When did that happen?" Poppy asked.

"Two years ago," Marge replied.

"I wonder if they finally stopped putting people up there after the woman jumped? Hallsey said they had too many problems up there."

"There was no report as to why she jumped, she left no suicide note. The newspapers made a big deal out of her being frightened off by the ghost."

"Of course they would say that. It sells papers. Any more?" Doyle asked.

"That's it. I think the hotel has had its share of problems," Marge said.

"Thanks, Marge. That just gets my curiosity going," Poppy said.

"You really are going to the hotel on the full moon?" Marge asked.

"Yep, I may even want to stay in room 504."

"Is that the room where Jane hung herself and her lover was found?" Marge asked.

"It is. I want to really stir up the ghost to get her to show herself," Poppy said with a grin.

"Well, have fun," Doyle said. "I'll be in another room watching,"

Doyle's Haunting

"Coward. You've been in law enforcement for a lot of years, seeing dead people and rousting criminals, and you can't stand up to one little ghost?"

"I can explain dead bodies and criminals, but ghosts are another matter."

Marge laughed and said, "Arthur, you said you didn't believe in ghosts."

"I said that, before I started hearing all this ghost stuff. It makes me wonder."

"Well, we'll see soon," Poppy said.

"You do know that the full moon is on Halloween?" Marge asked.

"Yes, we do and it makes it all the better. Maybe we'll be visited by demons, too," Poppy laughed.

"I shot the last demon I want to see. Skeeter's death was my Halloween treat," Doyle said. "I'm worn out for the day climbing around on a five story hotel roof. Let's call it a day and go home to relax?"

"It is almost closing time, anyway," Marge said. "I have nothing else to report and no clients came in today."

"That settles it, we go home. Oscar," Doyle called back to the man, "are you ready to hit the bricks?"

"I have one more report to file, then I'll head out."

"Okay, see you in the morning," Doyle said and stood. Poppy followed him up and they both said their goodbyes to Marge and went out the back door. They stood by Doyle's car and waited for Marge to come out. "I want to be sure she gets to her car safely," Doyle said.

"I'm sure she can handle any mugger," Poppy replied.

"I'm not worried about her, I'm worried about the muggers," Doyle laughed.

Marge came out of the building, waved and left. Poppy went to her car and followed Doyle out of the parking lot.

They arrived at Doyle's apartment and went in. "Any good spooky movies on TV tonight?" Poppy asked.

"I've had enough ghost stories for the day. Let's watch a good action movie with lots of gunfire."

Doyle's Haunting

"Actually, I think I'll take a shower. That attic was too dusty for me."

"Good, I'll join you." He followed her to the bathroom.

They had TV dinners and watched a couple sitcom comedies, then went to bed.

"Do you really believe we'll find Frobush's ghost?" Poppy asked with her head on her pillow.

"I don't want to think about it just before I sleep. I have bad enough dreams without having her floating through them." He paused, then said, "I still don't believe in ghosts, but there has to be something to it. I guess I'll get my proof Friday night."

They both slept fitfully. Doyle was awake a number of times, as was Poppy. They both decided around seven in the morning to get up.

Poppy said she had to go into work to report on the mystery room. "Since Hallsey called my boss, he wants to know about it. Otherwise I wouldn't have mentioned it. I'll just say it's storage with nothing harmful."

"What about Winfield's claim?"

"I'll say I'm still investigating the incident. But if we don't find a ghost then I'll report that she just fell because of carelessness and a loose carpet."

They dressed and headed out, Poppy to her job and Doyle to his office. Doyle came in and found Marge at her desk, Oscar was talking to her.

"Good morning," Doyle said to them.

"Did you sleep well, Arthur?" Marge asked.

"Not really, but I'll survive. Are we ready to start our day?"

Oscar said, "I have a case to go on. Something new, involving theft of goods from a store backroom. It's an electronics store and it seems they keep coming up short of gadgets. I'll go in as a new employee and see what I can find out."

"That sounds better than following cheating spouses. Think you can wrap it up soon? I may need you to help find a ghost."

"I'm sure it will be simple. I'll check out the employees and see which ones are unsavory. I'll be available to help you. I have to go to my job now, talk later."

Doyle's Haunting

Oscar went out and Doyle sat at his desk. "If anyone comes in today tell them to come back Monday, if it's not pressing. I hope I survive tomorrow night and don't get murdered by a ghost."

"I highly doubt you'll be murdered. Maybe frightened to death, but never murdered by a ghost. In my travels on the internet, I never saw one example of murder by ghost. Most people die from fright, not being attacked by a ghost. That looks good in a movie, but not in real life."

"Yeah, well if I come in Monday and I have white hair, you'll know I was frightened."

*

Chapter 17

"You're getting a little grey already, Arthur."

"Thank you for reminding me. I'll pick up some hair color this weekend," he grinned.

The back door opened and Poppy walked in. Doyle said, "That didn't take very long. Did you satisfy your boss?"

"Don't say it like that. I'd just as soon satisfy a camel before him. I went in, wrote my report and left before he saw me. I'm fast."

"Yes, fast and loose," Doyle said with a grin.

She hit his shoulder and sat at his desk. Doyle sat and smiled. "What are we going to do until tomorrow night?"

"Do you need to ask?" she said with a smile.

"If you are referring to sex, I think we need to be at our best. So sex would just drag us down."

Doyle's Haunting

"Is that a sports excuse? No sex before a big game?" she asked.

"I didn't know you knew about those things."

"Hey, I read, and watch TV," she said.

"I'll remember that. As I said, what shall we do until tomorrow night?"

"Since Halloween is tomorrow and tonight is devil's night, there must be an all-night horror movie marathon playing on TV.

The office phone rang. Marge answered, "Doyle and Drew Investigations, how may I help you?" She listened then said, "One moment, please." She put the phone on hold and looked at Doyle. "Mr. Hallsey, for you."

Doyle thanked her and picked up the phone. He put it on speaker so Poppy could hear. "Mr. Hallsey, what can I do for you?"

"I called you because I needed to know if you have ever investigated psychic mediums before."

"I haven't investigated them recently, but when I was on the Detroit police force, I was in on a number of busts for fraud involving mediums. They took people for a lot of money and gave them a bunch of nothing in return. Why do you ask?"

"My employers felt a psychic would help in the case of Mrs.Winfield's lawsuit on the hotel. They hope the psychic can dispel the story of the ghost once and for all."

"I can see their concern, but Ms. Drake is an investigator and not a psychic. She would be more objective than a spiritualist in the occult arts."

"Well, this psychic is coming in today and I'd like you and Ms. Drake to keep an eye on her. I frankly don't believe in psychics, so I don't want to be alone with her."

"We'll be right over. Just ask her to relax in your lobby until we get there. Oh, and don't mention that we're investigators. If she's a real psychic, she should already know," Doyle said with a grin.

"Thank you, Mr. Doyle." He disconnected the call and Doyle looked at Poppy.

"Ghosts, demons and now psychics. This is going to be a great Halloween." He stood followed by Poppy. "I presume you heard all that, Marge?"

"I did, Arthur. My Mac would bust mediums for fraud when he was in Bunco."

Doyle's Haunting

"Bunco. That's a police term I haven't heard in a very long time. Now it's part of Vice."

"What's Bunco?" Poppy asked.

"Used to be a department of police to handle swindles, cheating, and deceit in things like psychics and other con games. Years ago, Sgt. Joe Friday and Officer Gannon on the TV show "Dragnet" would work out of the Bunco squad, busting some con artist for scamming some little old lady out of her life savings. It's a term not used anymore. Marge is old, so she uses old terminology."

"Arthur, I'm not that old," Marge said with a laugh.

"No, you aren't, Marge. Now, we'll go bunco on a medium at the hotel. Wish us luck that we don't end up contacting dead relatives. Hold my calls, especially ones from the dead," Doyle said with a grin.

Marge was laughing as Doyle and Poppy left the building.

They arrived at the hotel and went into the lobby. Hallsey was pacing the floor at the front desk. "Mr. Doyle, I'm glad you and Ms. Drake could come in so quickly. The psychic hasn't arrived yet."

"Good, when she gets here, tell her we're from your company to witness her findings. She may clam up if she knows we're investigators."

"I can do that. How does this psychic stuff work?" Hallsey asked.

"I watched one psychic ghost hunter work in a mansion in Detroit once. He was working with the police to show how these frauds work. The so-called psychic would first read up on as much as they can about the place they were working at. Old newspaper stories about any deaths in the building or reports of spirits. Then they would do something called 'cold reading' which is a term used by psychics and even mentalists during their shows. Basically they ask subtle questions or mention things and watch for reactions from the person they are giving a reading to. They are clever at leading people into giving answers that they would expand on, to make it look like they are getting word from a ghost."

Hallsey looked distressed. "Are all psychics fake?"

"Well, I have to believe that there may be people out there who have an ability to see things. The police around the world have worked with such psychics to help with cases. They find lost children and locate dead bodies. I don't have an answer how, but there are a lot of strange things going on out there."

Doyle's Haunting

"Like ghosts," Poppy said.

"Okay, I'll give you that. I still don't believe in ghosts, but who's to say they don't exist," Doyle answered her. He turned back to Hallsey, "You haven't been working here very long, especially since the ghost started haunting, so you don't need to give this psychic any information. My secretary did some research on this hotel and had some interesting things to say about it. We'll know if she's telling the truth or blowing smoke."

"That will be so good. Mrs. Winfield is having fits about her lawsuit, and I got a call from her lawyer about our progress. I stalled him, but we need answers about this ghost story and her fall."

"We can't say much until tomorrow night during the full moon," Poppy said. "If we actually see the ghost, then she has a case. My determination is she was just careless, but I have to follow up on her claim."

"My employers called me this morning about sending in this psychic. So I have to let her do what she needs to do. I'll tell her you two are from the company to take notes as to her findings."

"Perfect. We should be able to give you our opinion after she is finished," Doyle said just as the front entrance door opened and in came a woman, about thirty, blondish hair and a little overweight. She had a haughty air about her, like she knew something you didn't. She had half glasses sitting low on her nose with cords attached going around her neck. She was accompanied by a smaller man dressed in black. They came to Hallsey as he approached them.

"Are you Sylvia Platt?" Hallsey asked.

"I am, and you are?" she snottily replied.

"I'm Roderick Hallsey, manager of the hotel. I was told you were coming."

"Fine, let's get this started," she said and walked past him.

*

Chapter 18

The woman walked up to Doyle and Poppy and stopped. Hallsey came up quickly and said, "These people are from the company that hired you. They are here to take notes of your findings. This is Mr. Doyle and Ms. Drake."

The woman just stared. Doyle almost felt she could read his mind the way she was looking at him.

"Miss Platt, my company requires me to ask you about your qualifications. Just to be sure they'll receive a legitimate reading," Doyle asked. "As you may already know, a lawsuit is in the works and if this comes to trial, we need to know your experiences."

She continued to stare, and then said, "What is your position at your company?"

"Well, my position is of no concern, I'm just here to report what you find. I need to know if you can do the job."

"I'm fully qualified. I've been on television giving my readings to millions of people on a weekly basis. I have been tested under rigorous conditions by many universities and I have helped a number of police departments across the country in finding victims of crime. Your company should already know these things."

"I'm sure they do, but I was given the task of being sure we get a proper reading. So please don't take offense, it's my job."

She didn't say much more to Doyle. She turned to Hallsey, "Lead me to the haunted floor, please."

Hallsey scooted towards the elevator and motioned her and her companion in. Doyle said they'd meet them up there and went for the stairs.

"I'm going to be worn out climbing the stairs," Poppy said.

"It's good for you. This woman is just plain spooky herself."

"She does seem to have a stick up her butt. I guess she believes her own press," Poppy replied as they reached the third floor.

"She didn't say anything about our vocations. Maybe we don't look like investigators."

"You look like a salesman."

Doyle's Haunting

"I do? Well, you'll have to dress me better, then," he said as they reached the fourth floor, where Winfield was staying.

Poppy looked down where the woman claimed she was pushed. "I still say she was clumsy."

"Maybe the psychic will tell us that," Doyle said as they went up to the fifth floor. "That elevator isn't very fast." He looked out to the cage moving slowly up. They got to the fifth floor and waited.

Hallsey opened the gate to let them off. He waited for Platt and her man to exit. The woman moved to the center of the hallway and was acting strange. She was turning around slowly and holding her hands out away from her body.

"There's death here, I can feel it," she mumbled low, then repeated herself.

Doyle and Poppy went down the hall a bit and watched. "I'm sure most people know there is death on this floor," Doyle said quietly.

The woman was now touching the walls and moving from door to door feeling the wood. "Yes, tragic death here. So sad, a love lost in a horrible murder. The pain I feel from a woman who loved the victim. She couldn't bear to be away from him. She took the way of suicide to join her love in the hereafter." She was still talking aloud.

"If she went to see her love in the hereafter, then why is she still haunting the place?" Doyle said to the woman.

Platt snapped her head towards Doyle. "I sense you are a disbeliever, Mr. Doyle."

"I'm a skeptic, yes."

The woman smiled and went on. She was still touching doors and stopped at room 504. She proclaimed, "This is the room where the two of them died. May I go in?"

Hallsey took out his passkey and unlocked the door. The woman entered, followed by her companion, then Hallsey.

Doyle said to Poppy, "That was no surprise. The room number has been reported ever since the deaths." They followed them in the room. It was the first time Doyle or Poppy were in that room. It felt cold.

"Yes, there's a chill in this room, the spirit is restless. She wants to find the killer of her lover, so she waits here for his return. I can feel her in the room. She's telling me something but it's hard to hear. She's not happy there is a disbeliever in the room," she said and eyed Doyle out of the corner of her eye.

Doyle's Haunting

"Do you want me to leave so you can talk to Janice?" Doyle asked.

"No, stay, I'll calm Janice down," the woman replied.

"Why don't you ask her what her name is?" Poppy said.

"I'm being told its Janice Freburg," the woman said.

"Why don't you try Jane Frobush? That's her name," Doyle said.

The woman looked confused. "Maybe I misunderstood her. It's hard to hear under these conditions."

"What conditions? My being a skeptic?"

Platt ignored Doyle and acted like she was going in a trance. "I'm communicating with the ghost of Jane. Please be silent." She shook her body and then said, "Jane will haunt on the next full moon and take revenge on someone in the hotel. So beware." She stood straight and said, "That's all I have. She's gone now."

Platt went out of the room followed by the man, who never spoke. Hallsey looked frustrated and followed. Doyle looked to Poppy, "That was one of the worst ghost readings I've ever seen. Even the guy who helped the police did better and he admitted he was a fake."

They followed them out and Hallsey led the woman to the elevator. Doyle and Poppy took the stairs.

On the ground floor the woman said she was satisfied that she contacted the spirit. "You can report to your superiors that there is a ghost trapped in this building." She turned and went out the front door followed by her companion.

Hallsey turned to Doyle in a panic. "What do I tell my employers? I can't say we actually have a ghost because that nutjob woman said so. Winfield's lawsuit depends on a ghost pushing her. If I say that's what happened, people won't be happy."

"Mr. Hallsey, the ghost is supposed to come out tomorrow on the full moon. Platt even said that. So we'll hang around the fifth floor and watch. If there is no ghost it will make Platt look like a fraud and Winfield will have no case. So let us come in and wait for Frobush to appear."

"I guess I'll have to trust you. So far you've been very helpful about everything else. I do appreciate it."

"No problem. We'll be back, and if your company calls, just say that the psychic is coming back tomorrow night to have a séance. That should keep them happy. We'll be back."

Doyle and Poppy left the building and back to the car. "I'll be glad when this is over. That woman was annoying. I don't see how she's some big shot psychic," Doyle said.

"I hope she wasn't charging for that fiasco. She didn't even get the name of Jane right."

"That's why I called her Janice," Doyle said, "to see if it would throw her off."

"Well, it did. Now what do we do for the rest of the day?" Poppy asked.

"Let's go see if we can find an all-night horror marathon on TV," Doyle grinned.

*

Chapter 19

"It's Devil's Night," Doyle said. "Maybe we should stay in the office to catch kids trying to soap the windows."

"When was the last time your windows were cleaned?" Poppy asked as they drove back to the office.

Doyle paused and thought. "I don't remember them ever being cleaned. I'll have to call someone."

"Well, I don't think soaping the windows will hurt them. You can take a bucket of water and give them a good cleaning."

"Sometimes they use wax instead of soap, just to be mean," he said.

"Just be glad the little gangsters in your neighborhood don't throw rocks."

"Very true. Let's go get some food. I'm hungry," Doyle said as he steered the car into the parking lot of Wong's Garden Restaurant.

Doyle's Haunting

"I guess we'll have Chinese?" Poppy grinned

They went in and had a good meal, then relaxed.

"Do you really think we'll see a ghost?" Doyle asked as he fiddled with his fortune cookie.

"Ask your fortune cookie," Poppy replied.

He broke it open and read the small slip of paper. "It says 'Help, I'm held prisoner in a fortune cookie factory.' How quaint."

"That's not what it says. That joke is so old it's not funny anymore. What does it really say?"

Doyle read it again and said, "Your future is in the hands of someone who will appear to you soon. Listen to them carefully." He put the paper down and Poppy took it to read.

"It's about Jane Frobush. She's going to appear to you soon. She should have a message for you."

"Yes, she'll tell me to find another girlfriend."

"She better not say that or I'll shoot her."

"You can't shoot a ghost, they're already dead."

"I'll figure out something."

"You think about that while I pay for the food and we'll go."

They went out to the car as it was just getting dark. Poppy's cell phone buzzed and she answered it.

"Hello, Poppy Drake here." She listened for a few moments, then said, "We'll be there immediately." She hung up and looked at Doyle. "Get back to the hotel. Winfield was murdered."

Doyle gave her a surprised look and started the car. They arrived at the hotel and saw police cars at the front entrance, along with the coroner's van and the crime scene van. Doyle parked across the street and they ran to the entrance where they were stopped by a patrol cop.

"We need to get in," Doyle said and brought out his badge. The cop looked at it and was confused.

"You aren't police," he said.

A voice from behind him called, "It's okay, Marty, I know them. Let them in." It was Marco Lupis, Doyle's friend.

"What are you doing here, Doyle?" Marco asked.

"We were investigating an accident claim for Poppy's company. How did Winfield die?"

Doyle's Haunting

"You knew Winfield?"

"She had a claim that Poppy was investigating. We talked to her and we're following it up."

Marco looked at Poppy. "Does he talk for you now?"

"I can't get a word in edgewise most of the time," she said. "I was investigating a claim that the Winfield woman was pushed down the stairs by a ghost. We were going to watch for the ghost tomorrow night."

"Why tomorrow night?"

"Full moon. It's when the ghost haunts the hotel. How was she killed?"

"Someone slit her throat. Quick and clean. She bled out. You did say a ghost?"

"You don't know about the Algonquin ghost?"

"I've heard a little about it. A spook running loose in these halls. This wasn't done by a ghost."

"Mr. Doyle, Ms. Drake, you came. Thank you." Hallsey came over and looked like he was on the verge of a heart attack.

"Roderick, what happened?" Doyle asked.

"I don't know. One of the housekeeping ladies went to see if Winfield needed new linens and found her in bed. Blood all over the place. I'm getting sick of this hotel. It's nothing but death. It should be burned down."

"Take it easy, Hallsey. Don't make claims that can get you into trouble," Marco said.

"I don't care, the last three days have been a nightmare. Now Winfield is dead, my employers are going to blame me for this, I just know it. I need a new job," Hallsey moaned.

Doyle felt sorry for the little man. He looked so pathetic standing there on the verge of tears. Doyle went to him and put his arm around the man.

"Roderick, we'll find the killer. So take a big breath and relax. You have the best private investigator in Detroit working for you now."

Marco snickered to himself. Doyle gave him a nasty look. "Marco, isn't there a donut with your name on it somewhere?"

"Doyle, I'm sympathetic to his feelings. You know as a former cop, we have to suspect everyone. I don't think Hallsey did it. But I don't believe a ghost did it, either. This was a human who committed this crime. Now, if you have any information, it will go better for him."

"We don't have anything that can help you, Marco," Doyle said. 'We're still investigating it ourselves. May we see the crime scene?"

Marco waved his hand to the stairs and they went up. Hallsey stayed below at Doyle's insistence. They reached the fourth floor and it was a flurry of cops, CSU and the coroner's men.

"Doyle, are you here to solve this murder?" asked Tom Sharp, the county coroner. Doyle had brief contact with the man in the past.

"Only if a ghost did it," Doyle replied.

"It's Devil's Night, Doyle, so you believe a ghost killed the woman?"

"Nope, the ghost only comes out on a full moon. Which is tomorrow night, Halloween."

"I've heard that story. Are you going to corral the ghost and get a confession?" Sharp said with a laugh.

Doyle studied the body of Winfield in bed with blood all around her. "The victim had her throat slashed? Just like the victim in 1945 in a room upstairs. The man whom the ghost hung herself over." Doyle said.

"Yep, the story is well known in the annals of crime. It was never solved and the poor woman killed herself for love. What a waste," Sharp responded.

"You've never been in love, Tom?" Doyle asked.

"It's a great waste of time and energy. I like one night stands. No commitments and no moony women following you."

"You just tell them you're the coroner and they'll stop following you," Doyle said with a smirk.

"It's a great ice breaker, Doyle. I'm sure a big macho private dick like you has a string of women."

"He better not," Poppy said, coming forward. "I lay claim to his body."

Sharp's mouth dropped slightly at the sight of the gorgeous woman. "Well, you have good taste, Doyle."

"No, I have good taste," Poppy said, with an evil grin.

"Can we stop outdoing each other?" Marco exclaimed. "What have you found out, Sharp?"

"She was killed with what could be a straight razor. She bled out quickly, her carotid artery was cut. She was dead in minutes. Whoever did this came from her right and slit across from left to right. She had to have known the person. There were no signs of a struggle. Unless the killer was invisible, she didn't defend herself."

"Invisible like a ghost?" Marco said with a laugh.

*

Chapter 20

"The ghost didn't do this, Marco," Doyle said. "We're on the fourth floor, the ghost only haunts the fifth floor."

"Maybe he's branching out," Marco said with a smirk.

"She. The ghost is a she," Doyle said. "Tom, about what time was she murdered?"

"I'd say between four and six. The room is a little chilly, so it could have affected the temperature of the body."

Doyle looked at Poppy and asked, "Why is it so chilly in here? I know this is October, but don't they turn on the heat?"

"I'll go ask Hallsey," she replied and went out of the room.

The leader of the crime scene people said, "It would be nice if you all would get out of the room until we're finished. Except you, Sharp."

Doyle and Marco went out and met with Hallsey, now upstairs. Poppy was beside him.

"I did say for you to stay downstairs," Doyle told Hallsey.

"I know, but there's one of Mrs. Winfield's relatives wanting to get in the building."

"Well, let's go meet him," Marco said. Everyone went back down the stairs to the lobby. They went to the entrance where there was a man standing with the cop guarding the door.

"He says he's her son," the cop said as Marco came up.

"Let's see some ID," Marco asked.

Doyle's Haunting

The man took out his wallet and produced his driver's license. Marco studied it and said, "Winfield was your mother?"

"Was? What do you mean 'was'? What's wrong and why are the police here? Is my mother all right?"

Marco nodded to the cop and he let him enter the lobby. Marco took the man aside and paused.

"Mr. Winfield, I'm sorry to tell you, your mother was murdered this afternoon."

He choked and said, "Murdered? How?"

"We're investigating that. Why did you come here at this hour?" Marco asked.

"I got a call from the hotel to come here. I didn't ask who called, they said they were from the hotel and I was needed. The person wouldn't tell me anything else."

Hallsey said, "Well, I didn't call him. I'll go find out who did." He went to the front desk to talk to the clerk.

They waited as Hallsey was conversing with the clerk. They finished and Hallsey came back. "It seems that Mrs. Winfield had filled out an 'in case of emergency' card to call her son, so my desk clerk called him, but didn't want to mention she was murdered. I didn't know she called."

"Okay, Winfield. How was your relationship with your mother? On good terms?" Marco asked pointedly.

"My God, are you suspecting me of murdering my own mother? Are you an idiot?" Winfield responded with shock.

"He is most the time," Doyle said quietly.

"Shut up, Doyle, or you can leave the building," Marco snapped. "Mr. Winfield, we have to suspect everyone, even someone like Doyle. He could have murdered your mother."

Winfield looked at Doyle with disdain, then said," I was with a dozen people today, all day. You can check this. It was a backyard Halloween party for children."

"Why today? Tomorrow is Halloween," Marco asked.

"Because tomorrow parents will be taking their children out early to trick or treat. It's too dangerous to go out after dark."

They stood there as Sharp and his men were bringing the body down to take to the morgue. Doyle watched Winfield as the gurney passed by. He seemed a little too calm for just losing his mother to murder.

Winfield turned to Marco and said, "May I go now? I'd like to follow my mother."

"So go, but stay handy. I'll be wanting to check your alibi," Marco replied.

Winfield gave him a dirty look and went out after the coroner's people.

"You should be a diplomat in Iraq. You have a lot of finesse," Doyle said.

"I suppose you didn't notice that he wasn't very broken up over mommy dearest being dead?"

"Yeah, he was awfully cool about it. Maybe you should look into the family jewels and see who inherits." Doyle said. "She had some pushy lawyers for her lawsuit against the hotel, so she must have some money."

"Lawsuit? What lawsuit?" Marco asked with renewed interest.

"She was suing the hotel for her injuries when she fell down the stairs. She said it was a ghost who pushed her," Poppy said.

"Interesting, maybe she was murdered by an employee of the hotel to screw up the lawsuit," he said eyeing Hallsey.

"I didn't kill her," Hallsey exclaimed. "I was with people all day. Guests and the staff. I was never alone. You can check."

"I may do that," Marco said. "Now, Doyle, are you and your girlfriend still pursuing this ghost tale? Since the old lady is dead, it's kind of moot now."

Poppy said, "Well, it's now a matter of curiosity to see if she did have a claim about a ghost pushing her. I'll still be here."

Doyle grinned and said, "What she said."

"You can chase ghosts all you want. I have to chase a killer. Keep me informed of anything you come across. I know you, Doyle, you'll hunt for the killer, too."

"Me. Never, it's your case. I know you'll find whoever did this horrible thing," he said with a straight face.

"Yeah, just keep me informed," he said and went to the stairs and up.

Doyle turned to Hallsey. "So, do you have any ideas who murdered her?"

Doyle's Haunting

"I have no idea. I didn't see anyone moving around her floor. We have only two other guests on that floor and I put them far away from Winfield because she would complain about noise."

"Who are they?" Poppy asked.

"Some salesman who is in town for a convention and a young couple on their honeymoon. Not exactly killers."

"Maybe they saw or heard something. Let's go talk to them," Doyle said.

"Shouldn't we wait until Marco has left?" Poppy asked.

"Yeah, he'd just get in the way. We can wait."

An hour later, the crime scene people had released the room and left. Marco took his men and told Doyle he'd be back. They left, so Doyle took Poppy over to Hallsey, who was helping some new guests. He was explaining why the police were there.

"It was a problem in one of our rooms. Nothing of which to concern yourselves with. We have a nice room on the ground floor so you don't have to climb the stairs," he told them.

Bob Moats

They agreed and signed in. Hallsey was looking nervous as he called for Andrew to take their bags to their room. The young man came up and led the couple to the room. Hallsey went to Doyle and Poppy.

"Now what?" he asked.

"Let's go visit the newlyweds, they're probably holed up in the room doing despicable things to each other."

"Like we do every night?" Poppy said quietly.

"Sure and we aren't married, so it's not legal."

"Legal schmegal, you don't have to be a newlywed to do it," she replied.

Doyle laughed and told Hallsey to lead the way. They climbed the stairs again as Poppy complained again. They got to the room and knocked.

The door opened and a young girl wearing a towel and a smile said, "Do you have the ice I called for?"

*

Chapter 21

She was blond, very cute and looked to be about twenty. Poppy poked Doyle in the back as he was trying to talk. "I'm sorry, we're not here with ice. We're here to investigate a murder."

The girl looked shocked and nearly dropped her towel, but grabbed it before exposing parts better left hidden. "Murder? Where?" she asked.

"At the other end of the hall," Doyle said. "About six hours ago. We need to ask if you've been out of your room at all today?"

She was fumbling with the towel and said, "Can I put on some clothes?"

"Sure, I think that would be a good idea," Poppy said.

The girl reached for the door when she lost hold of her towel and it dropped to the floor, just as she was closing the door.

"Get an eyeful there, stud?" Poppy said to Doyle who had his mouth open.

"Well, she's a real blond," Doyle said holding in his laughter. Poppy whacked him.

A few seconds later the door opened and the girl stood in a robe. "Sorry about that," she said, looking embarrassed.

"No problem, may we come in?" Doyle asked.

She opened the door wide and stood back. Doyle, Poppy and Hallsey came in. The room was slightly disheveled like they were having sex everywhere. Doyle grinned and looked at Poppy. She wasn't grinning.

"Okay, to get to the point. There was a woman murdered earlier today who was staying down the hall."

"You mean that crazy woman that kept yelling at us when we would go out?"

"When was this?" Poppy asked.

"Just before she fell down the stairs. After that we didn't see her."

"Okay, today she was murdered, were you out of the room at all today?"

Doyle's Haunting

"Just once when we went for food in the dining room. They have great food here," she said.

"Thank you," Hallsey said.

"When did you go? What time?" Doyle asked.

She was thinking and then said, "It was around noon. Yes, noon. We wanted lunch, which was very good."

Hallsey thanked her again.

"Let's get past the food. Now did you see anyone wandering the hallway on this floor?"

"There was no one wandering that we saw," she said, just as a young man came out from the bathroom, also in a towel.

"Oh, sorry. I didn't know we had guests. Excuse me, I'll get dressed." He went back into the bathroom. The hotel room was one big room other than the bathroom, so it was the only place he could change. They sat waiting for him to come out. He came out shortly, also in a robe.

"Honey, these people are the police, there was a murder on this floor today," the girl said. Her new husband looked shocked.

"On this floor? I didn't hear anything," he said.

"First, we're not the police. I'm a private investigator and my lady friend is an investigator for an insurance company. You already know Mr. Hallsey, the hotel manager," Doyle explained.

"So what happened?" the girl asked.

"As far as we can determine, the woman had her throat slit by an unknown assailant sometime between three and six."

"That's disgusting. You don't know who did it?" the girl asked, looking dense.

"Uh, no. That's why we're asking. So, you two didn't see anyone wandering the hallway today?"

The young man spoke, "I heard a noise earlier and opened the door to see what it was. There was a man standing in the hall doing nothing, just staring at the last door, where the old lady lived."

"Did you get a look at his face?" Poppy asked.

"No, he never turned and I didn't want to be seen. I closed the door before he moved."

"How tall was he and was there anything about him you can tell us?"

"Dark hair, but mostly grey. Short, but not too short. About my height. He was thin, and had dark clothes on. That's all I remember. Then I closed the door," the young man said.

"What time was that?"

"It was about two-thirty. I looked at my watch."

"Even that helps. At least we know someone was watching her room." Doyle looked at Hallsey. "Do you have security cameras?"

"Just at the front desk. We can record guests checking in," Hallsey said. "Nothing on the floors. Too expensive to install."

"I should have asked that before. Were the cameras aimed out at the lobby?" Doyle asked.

"Yes, they are. So anyone coming in the front door would be recorded."

"So anyone coming in would have to go through the lobby?" Doyle asked.

"It's the only entrance," Hallsey replied. "There are emergency doors that go out, but a person can't enter through them."

"So this stranger came in through the lobby and no one saw him?" Poppy asked.

"It's possible. The front desk gets busy and can't keep track of everyone who comes in. We get lots of people coming in to visit guests and use the dining room. It's open to the public."

"How many people come in each day?"

"According to bookkeeping we sell about forty or fifty lunches each day around the same timeframe as the murder." Hallsey said.

"I guess we have a lot of video to check then, don't we?" Doyle said. "We're sorry to intrude on your honeymoon, but thanks for the info."

They stood and left the young couple alone. Back down in the lobby, Hallsey took them to the office where he showed Doyle the security setup. Doyle had him run the system back to around two o'clock. Hallsey did some fidgeting with the system and the video came to life. They sat watching people come and go, then around two thirty a man came in but his head was covered with a hoodie.

"I hate those damn hoodies. They should be banned," Doyle said. "He fits the description the kid gave us." They watched him head in the direction of the stairs and went out of the camera's vision. "We'll wait and see when he comes down. Cutting Winfield's throat should have spurted blood, so his front should have blood trace."

They watched and then saw the same man come across the lobby, but he rushed out only showing his back.

"Damn, couldn't see his front or his face," Poppy said.

"So, we still don't know who he is, or if he's the killer," Doyle moaned.

"Well, I think he is and he's not a ghost," Poppy said.

"Are we still going to come in and watch for the ghost?" Doyle asked.

"I plan on it. Winfield may be gone and her case is over, but I need to know if there was a ghost. Don't you have a need to find out?" Poppy asked.

"I guess I do. I've put off finding out, so I do need to see if there is a ghost. So we'll come in and watch."

"One night for a ghost, then we can solve who killed Winfield. Deal?"

"Okay, deal," Doyle said. "Do we need to talk to the salesman on the floor?"

"He's never in," Hallsey said. "I suspect his convention is keeping him busy."

Doyle looked at Poppy. "A salesman in town for a convention? Probably left his wife at home, so I don't think he's going to hang around his room very often. We can forget about him."

*

Chapter 22

"Hallsey, did Ms. Drake ask you about the chilly temperature in Winfield's room?" Doyle asked.

"She did. Winfield insisted on it being cooler in her room. So, I had the vents closed off in there. I had hoped she'd get pneumonia and die. Sorry, that's not a nice thing to say."

"Under the circumstances, I understand your feelings. At least you didn't murder her that way," Doyle said. "Call Detective Lupis and tell him about the video and what the newlyweds said, that should keep him happy."

"Will they be back? The police I mean?" Hallsey asked.

"I'm sure Lupis will be back for more questioning. He only went off to get more facts from the ME and forensics before he digs into people's stories," Doyle explained.

Hallsey let out a deep sigh and said, "I'm going to find another hotel to work at. I can't take much more of this."

"Hang in there, Roderick, you'll be fine in a couple days after the full moon," Doyle told him.

"But, what about the full moon next month and the month after that," he moaned.

"One moon at a time, my friend. We just have to get through this moon."

Poppy said, "Now with Winfield dead, there's no reason to watch for the ghost."

"You're not getting out of it that easily. You started this ghost stuff and you're going to see it through. I'm wanting to prove there are no ghosts, and this is the perfect way to do it. We have a guaranteed ghost haunting coming up and I plan on being there."

"Good for you, tell me all about it if you survive."

"No, you and Oscar are both coming with me tomorrow night," he said.

"Great, drag Oscar into your fantasy."

"Stop that. You started this, let's finish it. Even if Winfield is dead. Damn, maybe she'll haunt the place now."

"That just gave me a chill. Can we go now?" Poppy said.

They said their goodbyes to Hallsey and walked briskly out to the car. Doyle drove back by the office. "I want to see if the windows were soaped," he said.

He drove by the front of the building and they could see the windows were untouched. "Good, now I can sleep better."

Back at Doyle's apartment, they relaxed on the couch. Doyle said, "This has been a busy week. Between all the ghost stuff, finding Skeeter still alive, shooting him and now the death of Winfield, I've had enough. To make matters worse, I'm going to watch for a ghost just to prove they don't exist."

Doyle's Haunting

"And if you see the ghost, will you admit they exist?"

"If I do, I will admit it. Although, I highly doubt it. Now, can we talk about anything else but ghosts?"

They heard a noise in the hallway and Doyle went to see what it was. He looked through the peephole and could see two young boys running around the hallway. He banged on the door to scare them, then carefully opened the door. They were gone now, but Poppy was laughing. Doyle looked back at her pointing to the door. He looked down and saw that they had spray painted a huge "BOO!" on the door in red.

"They couldn't have soaped the door, no, they had to spray paint it. Great, I'll call the building super and let him know." He stepped out in the hallway and looked at the other apartment doors. The little devils had hit all the doors. Doyle laughed now and went back in.

"Devil's night in Detroit used to mean setting fires to buildings. It was a mess and kept the fire departments running all night. There are sick people out there, Poppy."

"I know, I have to deal with them all too many times in my investigations of insurance fraud."

Doyle's cell phone buzzed and he looked at the caller ID, it was Oscar. He put the phone on speaker.

"What's up?" Doyle asked.

"I solved the store theft case," Oscar said. "Two stock boys were slipping gadgets out in the trash for their accomplices to cart away. Got the police involved and they were busted. I charged the store good for the stake out."

"Great, extra income is always nice. So, you'll be free to go chase a ghost tomorrow night?"

Oscar went silent. "Are you still there?" Doyle asked.

"I'm thinking of an excuse for being elsewhere," he replied.

"You just made your plan to be with us. Besides, I may need protection."

"What? You're going to push me in the way if the ghost attacks you. Is that plan B?"

Doyle laughed thinking about plan B. "I could dress you as a mummy like we did back during the hostage situation with the mayor."

"No, thank you," Oscar replied. "I'm not crazy about being wrapped up again. One time was enough. Are you dressing for Halloween?"

"I haven't dressed for Halloween since I was ten. I'm not going to start now."

"You could go as Indiana Jones with the hat you bought," Poppy said.

"That may be a choice. I'll think on it. Where would I get a whip?"

"There's a bondage shop in Detroit on Woodward," Oscar offered. "They have lots of leather items."

"And how would you know?" Doyle asked suspiciously.

"No, I'm not into that. I had to investigate a robbery back when I was with robbery division. We had to go check it out."

"Okay, I'll give you that. I just don't ever want to see you come into work wearing spiked heels and a bustier."

"I don't have the shape for it," Oscar laughed and said he had to go.

"Okay, see you tomorrow at work," Doyle said and hung up.

"What are you dressing as?" Doyle asked Poppy.

"I was thinking of Elvira, Mistress of the Dark," Poppy smiled evilly.

"Oooh, I could go for that."

"Only if you can dress up like George Clooney," she said.

"What happened to Indiana Jones?"

She thought for a moment and then said, "Okay, I'll give you that."

*

Chapter 23

They were up early anticipating the evening, but first they had to get through the day.

"After you're dressed, we'll go. I want to get an early start trying to find out what happened to Winfield," Doyle said.

"Why don't you let Marco work on it? You need a break," Poppy replied.

"I feel like we've gone through all this because of Winfield. So as much as I didn't like her, I feel an obligation to give her a proper send off."

"To the hereafter?" Poppy laughed.

"Wherever, just to get her out of our lives. Besides, I hate leaving a case unsolved. Now get dressed," Doyle said, then went to put his guns in their holsters and cover them with his jacket.

Poppy came out ten minutes later, dressed. "I'm ready." She gave Doyle a kiss for luck, she said.

They arrived at the office twenty minutes later, and found Marge talking to Marco. Oscar hadn't come in yet, judging by his empty chair.

"I watched the video this morning and talked to the newlyweds, it didn't help much, but we know it's a man. I'm having Winfield's financials being poked at and having her will checked over closely. Someone is trying to blame your ghost for this." Marco said.

"Have you talked to her son again?" Poppy asked.

"No, I'm heading there this morning. I wondered if you wanted to tag along."

"Are you saying you need my help?" Doyle said with a grin.

"Don't hold your breath, I can do this without you. I've solved lots of cases without your help. I heard from Marge that Skeeter resurfaced."

"He's dead now. We found him hiding in his house in a panic room down in the basement. He made the mistake of facing off with me," Doyle smiled.

Marco looked at Poppy, "I don't see a scar, so Doyle didn't wound you?"

Doyle's Haunting

"No, he's been practicing, or so he said. I just held my breath and waited for the shot," Poppy replied.

"Best not to move when Doyle fires his gun. Now shall we go roust the son a bit?"

Poppy stopped Doyle and said, "I really have to go back to my office and file my report concerning Winfield's death. I just hope I don't run into my boss. I'll call you later."

"Don't forget our adventure tonight. I don't want to have to track you down." He kissed her and she left the building.

"I don't know how you find them, Doyle. Good looking with brains, you are very lucky."

Doyle just smiled and said to go. "Marge, tell Oscar I expect him to go with me to watch for the ghost tonight."

"I will Arthur, I'd like to come also, but I get lots of kids trick or treating and I've already bought the candy," she said.

"Don't worry about it. I'll fill you in tomorrow. If I survive." He turned and led Marco out the back door. Marco said to take his unmarked car, in case they had to arrest someone.

Marco drove out and Doyle asked, "Do you know where to go?"

"I checked the computer for his location. I have a good idea where he is." They drove out to East Pointe, formerly East Detroit, and found the street. "It should be on the right side, 12896." They went down the street and found the house. Nothing exciting, just a plain, suburban ranch-style home. It looked like all the other houses on the street.

Marco parked and they went up to the house. It was all dressed up for Halloween, complete with fake tombstones on the front lawn.

"It amazes me how some people get so involved in Halloween. The religious fanatics cast off the day as worship for the devil. Stupid."

"Yet, those same people give a whole holiday to their savior. Who do you believe?" Marco said.

"I'd rather play with the Satan worshipers, they have more fun," Doyle laughed.

Marco knocked on the door and after a few minutes it opened. A woman, about fifty, plain looking in a housecoat, stood staring at them. "What do you want? I hope you're not selling anything," she grumbled.

Doyle's Haunting

Marco held up his badge and said, "No, ma'am, police matter, is your husband home?"

"What do you want that worthless piece of crap for? Are you going to arrest him?" she muttered, sounding like she drank her breakfast.

Doyle looked sideways at Marco, he was trying not to laugh. "No, ma'am, unless you know some reason we should?"

"I can give you a dozen reasons, but it would get me in trouble, too. He's not here."

"May we talk to you, then?"

"I guess so, I got nothing to hide. Come in," she sputtered and held the screen door opened.

Marco and Doyle went in and she took them to the living room. It was a disaster. Like someone had tossed it looking for something of value.

"Mrs. Winfield, did you have a break-in?" Marco asked.

"This mess, hell, no. This is what I have to put up with every day. I clean and my little bastard sons terrorize it. They started early this morning, Halloween is coming and they're practicing to be demons. Not that they need to practice. My idiot husband doesn't lift a finger to punish them, he's always too busy dreaming ways to make a fortune."

Marco looked to Doyle with interest. "What does he dream up?"

"You name it. Any stupid scheme to make money. Selling soap products to stealing car parts to sell. I hope you take him away along with those little bastards we call our children."

"Well, we would have to catch him committing a crime. Now do you know anything about his mother being murdered?"

The woman looked stunned. "What the hell? When?"

"Yesterday, around three in the afternoon. Do you know where your husband was during that time?"

She did some thinking and said, "We had a Halloween party in the back yard. Paul said he had to go get some refreshments and was gone for over two hours. I know he didn't want to be involved in the party, leaving it all up to me to supervise ten screaming little monsters. He came back and didn't have any refreshments but he rushed into the house. I followed him and he was changing clothes. I was fed up with him and told him he could watch the kids. I went to my room and locked the door."

Doyle's Haunting

"The clothes he was wearing when he came back, do you still have them?"

"If you want to dig through the pile of clothes, go ahead and find them. I haven't done laundry yet. Come with me, I'll show you." She stood and they followed her to a laundry room. There were two big piles of clothes on the floor. She pointed to one and said, "That's from yesterday."

Marco said, "I should get CSU in here to examine this. I'll make an emergency call." He pulled out his cell phone and called dispatch.

They waited for the team to show but Marco dug a little and found a hoodie jacket. It had blood on the front. He carefully put it back and stood up. "We got him. Now I'll let CSU bring it out. Just to make it official."

"You're such a good cop, Marco."

"It's a curse," he laughed.

*

Chapter 24

They waited for the forensic people to come, just as the side door opened and in came Winfield. He came by the laundry room yelling, "Honey, I'm home." He looked to his right, into the laundry room and saw Marco and Doyle.

He stopped and said, "What the hell? What are you doing in here?"

"Mr. Winfield, you are under arrest on suspicion of murder of your mother. You have the right to remain silent," he gave Winfield the rest of the Miranda as Winfield protested. Doyle held on to him as Marco put the cuffs on him.

"You can't do this, I have rights," he was screaming.

Marco spun him around. "You lied to us yesterday. You said you were here all day, but your wife said you left for a couple hours, then came home to change your clothes. I've got forensics coming to dig through your laundry. If they find a Hoodie with blood on it, you will be charged with murder."

Doyle's Haunting

Winfield went silent and said, "I want a lawyer."

"As you wish," Marco replied. They heard a knock at the front door. Mrs. Winfield said she'd get it. A few moments later the CSU men came in. Marco explained what they were looking for, even though he already knew, but didn't say. Marco and Doyle took Winfield out of the laundry room and to the living room.

Shortly, the supervisor of the CSU came out with a large plastic bag containing the hoodie. "It was in the pile, like you said it might be. There's blood trace all over the front. We'll compare it to the dead woman and get the results to you."

"Thanks, Steve," Marco turned to Winfield as the CSU men left. "I'm satisfied that you killed your mother. Not a nice thing to do, Paul."

"Screw you. She was a miserable old bitch. She was rich and wouldn't loan me any cash to front my businesses. I figured they'd blame the ghost for killing her, the one she said pushed her. She was a scam artist, too. She knew the story of the ghost and made up that excuse to file a lawsuit against the hotel. She told me that when I went to see her last week."

Marco smiled at Doyle, "You can tell Poppy about this revelation. There was no ghost involved."

"I'm still making her go watch for it tonight. It's something we need to prove to ourselves."

"Yeah, well, don't get murdered," Marco laughed, and they took Winfield out to the car. Marco dropped Doyle off at his office and sped off. Doyle watched him go just as Poppy drove in. She got out of her car and went to Doyle.

"Got some good things to tell you. Let's go in so I can share with Marge and Oscar," he said and they went in.

Marge was talking on the phone when Doyle and Poppy came in. Oscar was rummaging in the storage room. He came out when they entered.

"I was looking for that catalog of security devices that I got a couple months ago when we were protecting ourselves from Skeeter. Have you seen it?" Oscar asked.

"It's in my desk drawer, bottom right. Help yourself. Thinking of buying something?" Doyle asked.

"An alarm system for my apartment. There have been a number of break-ins recently and I want to be ready." Oscar replied.

Doyle went to his desk and opened the drawer, allowing Oscar to reach the catalog. He took it back to his desk and sat. Marge hung up her phone and smiled at Doyle.

"Sister again?" Doyle asked.

Marge laughed and said, "Yes, she hasn't been as bothersome lately, so I tolerate a short call once in a while. How did your visit with the son go?"

"Well, he did murder his mother," Doyle said.

"See, the ghost didn't do it," Poppy smirked.

"He also said that his mother told him that she made up the whole ghost pushing thing. He said she was a scammer. It runs in the family, from what I heard. Winfield's wife was more than happy to turn her husband in."

"Marriage is a wonderful prison," Oscar said from his desk.

Doyle laughed and said, "Now, we have to get ready to go spend the night in the hotel for ghost watching."

"Hey," Oscar exclaimed, "you didn't say anything about staying overnight."

"Well, we won't see the ghost until around midnight, or so they say. We may as well stay. It would be nice to sleep in a new place," Doyle said.

"You slept in your rebuilt cabin, which was new," Poppy said.

Doyle paused, thinking. "Yes, we did. Okay, this is another new place. May as well take advantage of the free offer for a room."

"Hopefully Hallsey will still be working there," Poppy said. "He was pretty upset about the last few days. I hope he doesn't quit."

"Or get fired. His employers don't sound very nice. I hope he doesn't mention anything to them about Winfield for a couple days. Just until we can verify the ghost legend."

"The company may not like him withholding that info," Poppy said. "I'm sure he's already told them that the lawsuit is no longer in effect."

"Speaking of that, did you report to your boss that Winfield's claim is now no longer a problem?"

Poppy grinned and said, "I did and he was glad to be rid of it. He didn't thank me for all my hard work on this claim, but at least he wasn't snotty about it."

"You know you always have a job here, if he gets too snotty," Doyle said with a laugh.

Doyle's Haunting

"I'm not wanting to work with you then go home with you," she replied. "Too much time together."

"Yes, that can kill a romance." Doyle looked at his watch and said, "Shall we go get ready for the big night?"

Oscar grumbled something, then said louder, "Are we meeting here and what time?"

"Eight sharp will be fine. Be here and bring your camera. We may need photos."

Oscar perked up on that note, "Yeah, I can try out my new lens I got for spying on cheating spouses. It's for low light and should pick up a ghost easily enough."

"Good, we'll meet here at eight then." Doyle looked at Marge, "have a nice night with your trick or treaters."

"I will and I may take some pictures also," she said.

"Good. Well, we are done here," Doyle said to Poppy and they left.

Oscar gathered his things and walked Marge out to her car.

"See you in the morning, Oscar," she said.

"I hope so," Oscar said, frowning.

*

Chapter 25

Doyle and Poppy relaxed in his apartment, talking.

"I think we have a good relationship. We get along, we goof around and we're great in bed," Doyle said.

"I don't think that's any reason to move in together. That would be like getting married," Poppy replied. "You've avoided the mention of marriage a number of times. You aren't ready for that."

"I had a happy marriage once. I miss it."

"Yes, you and your late wife were a perfect match. It's hard to find that in a relationship."

"I think you and I are almost a perfect match," Doyle said with a grin. "On a scale of one to ten, I'd say we are an eight and a half."

"Eight and a half? Is that the best you can do?" she said, with a frown. "Can't you do better than that?"

"So where do you put us on a scale of one to ten?"

"Let's not dwell on it," she said.

"Wait. Are you not happy with me?"

"I am. You're a ten on the happy scale."

Doyle paused thinking about that. "Okay, I'll take it."

"Can we discuss moving in together later, like in a couple months?" she said.

"Okay, so I'm rushing things. You're right, we hardly know each other. So we'll take it slow and I'll wait for you to be ready. Is that acceptable?"

"Deal. In the meantime we can still have great sex and drive each other crazy," she said, with a grin.

"Deal. Now let's get ready to go hunt down a ghost."

"Do we really have to?" Poppy asked.

"This was your idea in the first place. I didn't want to go there. Now I do, so get up and let's go meet Oscar at the office."

They stood and went to the door. Doyle opened it and they were startled by two small goblins.

"Trick or Treat!" they yelled.

Doyle glanced at Poppy and said, "I don't have any candy."

"Money," Poppy replied. "That always worked for me."

Doyle dug into his jeans and pulled out a wad of cash. "How much?" he asked her.

"A couple of fives would be nice, and you can afford it."

Doyle peeled off two fives, giving one each to the children.

They looked into their bags and said, "Wow, thank you, Mr. Doyle," then they ran off.

"They know you?" Poppy asked.

Doyle's Haunting

"Everyone in this building knows me. Let's go before the parents come begging."

They left the building and Doyle threw his overnight bag in the back.

"I need to get a bag packed for me," Poppy said.

Doyle drove to the office where they found Oscar standing next to his car. They drove up and Oscar came over to them.

Poppy opened her door to let Oscar get in. "I'm doing this under protest. If I get injured, I'm suing."

"I'll be your witness," Poppy said.

"Glad someone appreciates the magnitude of this evening. We're going into the underbelly of the devil and his minions," Oscar said.

"Do you mean those cute little yellow minions in that 'Despicable Me' movie?"

"No, I mean those little horned, red-skinned demons that will attack and rip the flesh from our bones," Oscar said trying not to smile.

Doyle drove out and over to the hotel. "Are you going to be a good boy in here or shall we make you sit in a time out?" Doyle asked Oscar.

"You annoy me sometimes, Doyle," Oscar said. "I don't know why I let you talk me into these things. I don't like ghosts or spooky hotels, and this hotel is spooky."

"Okay, I'll give you that. It is spooky, but that's because it's old. They took pride in building beautiful structures back then. But we're used to simple, square, plain buildings now. The ornate architecture that once was the keystone of majestic buildings is now lost to throwing up a building quickly and saving money."

Oscar was quiet for a moment as were Poppy and Doyle. "What do we do in there tonight?" Oscar asked finally.

"We sit and wait for the ghost to appear. We'll relax on the fifth floor and wait. That's all we can do."

"That doesn't sound too hard. If the ghost appears, do we have a place to run to?"

"Hallsey said he would let us have a room. I'll get one for you."

"I'm not sleeping alone in that hotel. I'll bunk with you two."

Doyle glanced at Poppy and smiled.

Doyle's Haunting

Doyle parked the car in the parking structure and they went into the lobby. It was dark out and the interior lights hadn't been turned on yet, giving the lobby a spooky appearance. Doyle went to the front desk and asked, "Is Mr. Hallsey in?"

The girl clerk said, "He's locked himself in his office, I hope he's all right. He has to turn on the lights."

"We'll go see what he's up to," Doyle said and the three of them went down the dark hall to Hallsey's office. Doyle tried the knob but it was locked. "Hallsey!" Doyle yelled and banged on the door. They got no answer.

Doyle took out his lockpicks again and worked on the lock of the door. It gave way and Doyle opened it.

They entered the cluttered office and saw Hallsey slumped back in his chair.

"Oh, no. I hope he didn't kill himself," Poppy moaned.

Doyle ran around the desk and checked him. "He's still alive." Doyle picked up a prescription bottle from his desk. "Nerve medicine," he said. "I think he overdid it."

Doyle pulled Hallsey up and shook him gently. "Roderick, hey, wake up." He tried again and Hallsey was starting to come around. Doyle looked over and saw a coffee machine. "Poppy, get him some coffee, please."

Poppy went to the machine and poured a cup from the pot. She took it to Doyle and handed it to him. Doyle tried to pour the coffee into Hallsey's mouth. He spit out the coffee and opened his eyes.

"Hey, that coffee is bad," Hallsey sputtered. "What are you trying to do? Poison me?"

"Wake up, Roderick. Are you all right?"

"Hell, no. I'm wanting to crawl into a shell and disappear."

Doyle sat him up and stood back. "Roderick, we solved the lawsuit problem for you. Your employers should be pleased."

"I don't know, I haven't called them yet," he moaned.

"Roderick, you're delaying the inevitable. You don't know how they'll react. I'm betting that they'll be pleased with the result."

Doyle's Haunting

He sat back and looked despondent. "I'm not a strong person. I was amazed that I made manager of this hotel. I tried my best, but this week has tested my nerves."

"Okay, Roderick. You should relax and let us take care of things."

"I'll trust you, Mr. Doyle. You've been honest with me."

"Thank you Roderick. I think you should come up to the fifth floor with us to watch for the ghost. Maybe it will give you a different outlook on life," Doyle said.

"Or death," Poppy muttered quietly.

*

Chapter 26

"Poppy, let's not be negative," Doyle grinned. "Oscar, help me get Roderick up and moving."

Oscar came around the desk and they helped the man stand. He was shaky, but held himself up.

"I was feeling anxious and figured the muscle relaxers would help. I may have overdone it," Hallsey said woozily.

"Well, we'll walk you around and I think climbing the stairs will do you a world of good," Doyle said as they walked Hallsey around the desk. "You also have to get the lights on. It's dark out."

"Oh, dear," he exclaimed and moved away from Doyle, going to a panel in the wall. "I told them they should automate the lights, but it would be too expensive, they said. Just another annoyance in my day."

They left the office and went out to the lobby. Andrew was standing by the front desk waiting to take a young couple to their room. He looked back and smiled.

Doyle's Haunting

Hallsey snapped up straight and went to the couple. "Welcome to the Algonquin Hotel, folks. I'm Mr. Hallsey, the manager, if you need anything, feel free to call the desk."

They agreed and Andrew took them away. Hallsey looked a little more invigorated now.

"We have a couple hours before midnight and the ghost, shall we get something to eat?" Doyle looked at Hallsey and asked, "Is your dining room still serving?"

Hallsey looked at his watch and said, "No, they stopped serving about an hour ago."

"Fine, I'll call out for pizza and we'll have a Halloween party." Doyle pulled out his cell phone. "I have my favorite pizza place, Cloverleaf, on speed dial." He called and ordered two large supreme pizzas and a couple two liter bottles of Pepsi.

Thirty minutes later the pizza arrived. They took the boxes and soda pop to the dining room and sat at a table. Doyle had Hallsey invite the staff to have a slice. Andrew and the girl at the front desk came and took some food.

They finished up and Doyle announced it was time to go watch for the ghost.

"Couldn't we just sit here and watch?" Oscar said with a grin.

"Up, Oscar. Let's go face our demons." Doyle, Poppy, Oscar and Hallsey went out to the lobby and over to the stairs. It was quiet in the hotel. Guests were probably out at some Halloween party or relaxing in their rooms.

They climbed up to the fifth floor and Hallsey asked what room they wanted to use.

"Any room, except 504, will be fine," Doyle said.

Hallsey went to 505 and took out his passkey, opening the door. "Just lock it when you're finished."

Doyle asked Oscar to help him take some chairs and the small couch out into the hallway. They set the furniture up facing the attic door which gave them a good view of room 504. Poppy sat on the couch and relaxed. Doyle sat next to her as Oscar and Hallsey sat in the chairs.

"Okay, now we sit and wait. Does anyone have a good ghost story to tell?" he said with a grin.

"Shall I start a campfire?" Oscar mugged.

"No, we didn't bring any marshmallows," Poppy added.

Doyle's Haunting

"I haven't been working here long enough to have had the chance of seeing the ghost," Hallsey spoke when it got quiet. "Seems I'm usually not here during the full moons. Maybe I was avoiding it."

"We all try to avoid things we don't understand," Doyle said. "Ghosts are something we only hear about, but never see. At least most of us," he said, looking at Poppy. "I tend to take stories of ghosts with a grain of salt. So hopefully this will put my mind at ease."

They sat staring at the doors to the room and attic. "Where is she going to come from? The room she died in or the attic?" Oscar asked.

"I'd presume from her room," Doyle said. "Or she just materializes out here. Who is she trying to haunt if there's usually no one up here during the full moon?"

"She's anguished over her lover's death. So she doesn't need people to haunt," Poppy spoke. "She just comes out to mourn the anniversary of his death."

"Every full moon? I hope she's not buying anniversary presents, that would get expensive." Doyle smirked.

Poppy gave him a dirty look, and continued. "It's so much more of a love story, two lost souls, locked

184

in the place where they died. She comes back hoping to find her lost love."

"So, where's he? Did he go to heaven or hell? Does he know she's wandering the halls every full moon? Why aren't they just getting together?"

"Well, if she was a religious person, suicide is a sin," Hallsey added. "Maybe they won't let her in heaven. Although, she wasn't a bad person from what I've heard."

"I'm sorry, Roderick, but I don't buy into all that. I think a person's essence, what you call a soul, leaves the body upon death and goes around until it finds a newborn whatever to inhabit, human or creature." Doyle said.

"So you believe in reincarnation?" Hallsey asked him.

"I understand that all matter doesn't just disappear, it just becomes something else. There's only so much matter in the universe and it keeps changing. Like a caterpillar, it morphs into a butterfly. Same matter, just reformed into a different shape."

Hallsey mulled that over. "Religion has everything explained in a neat package, so we don't have to think about things like death and where we go. It always frightened me growing up in a strict religious home. Behave or go to hell. Always that threat hanging over me."

"Maybe that's why you're such a nervous person," Oscar said.

"Very true," Hallsey agreed.

Doyle looked at his watch. "Twenty minutes until midnight, then we'll have our answer."

They sat quietly, just as Andrew came running up the stairs. "Mr. Hallsey! Come quick, there's a fire in the basement!" the young boy screamed and ran back down the stairs.

"Oh, no!" Hallsey yelled and jumped up, heading down the stairs.

"Let's go help," Doyle exclaimed and they followed Hallsey.

The hallway was now empty, just as there was a sound coming from the attic.

Herman had come up through his service elevator from the basement and rolled into his room. He picked up a small bottle on a table and then rolled to the massive door blocking his apartment from the attic. He reached up, unbolting the heavy locks and pushed open the door.

He left his little apartment and rolled through the attic, coming to the door leading to the hallway. He reached out and just barely touched the lock on the attic door. There were three short steps going down to the floor level, so it was a reach for him. The knob on the lock gave way to his twisting and he pushed open the door.

He saw furniture in the hallway and no one around. He smiled and carefully maneuvered down the short steps in his wheelchair. He reached the bottom and looked around. He saw no one, so he reached back and shut the attic door. The lock engaged and he knew he couldn't go back in, he had no key. But it didn't matter, he wasn't planning on going back in.

*

Chapter 27

Herman rolled out to the center of the hallway and checked his watch. It was now just before midnight. He opened the small bottle and drank the contents, then he threw the bottle down the hallway and waited. After a few minutes he felt dizzy, but he saw what he was waiting for. A shape was forming in front of him. It was just a dim haze and it came over to him.

The dim white light floated closer towards Herman, as he sat waiting in his wheelchair. He coughed a couple times and tried to focus his eyes on whatever was coming. He was sure it was the ghost of Jane Frobush.

"Hello, Jane," he spoke. "We finally meet. I've never come out on this floor, too many bad memories. I'm here now because there are changes coming to my life, and I have to settle some things. I don't know if you remember me? Back in 1945, I was a bellboy working here when you and your man came in to get a room. I thought you were the most beautiful woman I had ever seen."

Herman paused, thinking of words to say.

"After you two registered, I took you and your luggage to room 504. If I remember correctly, your man was named Ken Harlow, yes, that was it. He was a handsome man, but mean, I could tell. He didn't even tip me, the bastard. After I went out, I heard him yelling at you. Something about flirting with me. You didn't do that, you were just friendly. Then I heard him hit you. You let out a little yelp, but didn't cry out. I wanted to bust in and strike him hard. But he was bigger than I, so I didn't dare. I just waited and heard him hitting you again. It was all I could do to keep myself out of it. I finally left the floor and went back down to the lobby to do my job. All I could think about was that bastard hitting you."

Herman paused again, taking a deep breath. His lungs hurt and he was getting dizzy. He sat up and went on.

"I remember you were in town to sing at a local jazz club in the city. Harlow was your manager and lover. I wanted to go hear you sing, but I was too young to get in the club. I bet you were a great singer. The yelling and hitting kept up. I would sit on the stairs of the fifth floor and counted all the times he hit you. I hated him. One night you left to go to work, he stayed in the room. I waited until around midnight, then made my decision. I quietly used my pass key, slipped in and saw he was on the bed

Doyle's Haunting

sleeping. I had my father's shaving razor, which I got when he passed on. I went up to the bed quietly and ran the blade across his throat. His eyes opened and he tried to speak but couldn't. He grabbed my wrist and wouldn't let go. I pushed him away and stood back."

Herman took another deep breath and coughed hard.

"I stood there watching him die and I was glad. I had freed you from that monster. I suddenly heard someone at the door, probably you were coming back, and I panicked. I had nowhere to go so I climbed out the window and up to the roof. There was a full moon that night so I could see. I was moving over to a skylight when I slipped and fell to the pavement below. I lived, but that's why I'm in this chair."

He coughed harder now, holding a handkerchief to his mouth. He looked at it and there was blood.

"I'm sorry, Jane. I was taken to the hospital and never got out in time to see you again, before you took your own life. I never understood how you could have done that. Love does terrible things to us. I killed because I thought I loved you. You died loving him. Such a waste. Please forgive me, Jane."

He coughed very hard and his face went red. He slumped in his chair and was silent. The white mist came to him and surrounded him. The light slowly dimmed and finally faded.

~~*~~

In the basement, the fire was extinguished and everyone was checking to make sure it was out.

"Why this fire started will have to be determined by the fire marshal when they get around to it," Doyle said.

"Maybe the ghost started it," Oscar said.

"Damn, we forgot about the ghost," Poppy yelled. "What time is it?"

Doyle looked at his watch and said, "Just after midnight. Let's get back up there." They ran out of the room and up the stairs. They flew up the past the floors and finally arrived on the fifth floor. As they came up they saw Herman in his wheelchair.

"What the hell? Herman, what are you doing out here?" Doyle asked as they approached him. He didn't move, so Doyle checked his pulse. "He's dead," was all Doyle said.

Doyle's Haunting

"Oh, no. Why?" Poppy choked.

Doyle saw the envelope on Herman's lap and picked it up. He took out the paper and read it. "It's his confession to the murder of Jane's lover." He handed the handwritten letter to Poppy and said, "He committed suicide, by poison."

Poppy folded the letter back up after reading it all the way through. She was fighting the tears in her eyes as she said, "He explained why he killed the man. Herman must have suffered all these years being so close to the scene where he loved Jane and lost her. Then to be crippled because of that night. This is all so tragic."

An hour later, the coroner had taken Herman out as Marco was reading the letter. He folded it up and put it in the envelope.

"Well, this solves a sixty-nine year old cold case murder. I'll make my report and get back to you. Thanks."

"Hey, Marco, can we get a copy of that letter?" Doyle asked.

"Sure, I'll drop it off at your office. I'd like to say hi to Marge again." He smiled and went down the stairs.

Doyle turned to Poppy and Oscar, "We missed the ghost, but I think she was here with Herman. Why else would he be out here? He loved and lost."

"Love sucks," Oscar said. "I've been married three times and love didn't help any of those marriages."

"Some of the best love stories are the ones where the lovers can never get together. Romeo and Juliet for one," Poppy said.

"Yeah, and they killed themselves for love. As I said, love sucks. I'm going home. You two can make up great love stories about this night." Oscar went to the stairs and down.

"Do you really think Jane came out and met with Herman?" Poppy asked.

"He was out here, where she was supposed to be. I think he talked to her and professed his undying love, then passed on to the hereafter to see her again."

"Do you think she forgave him for killing her lover?" Poppy wondered, staring at the wheelchair still on the floor.

"I'd like to think she did, Harlow didn't sound like a nice person for her. Who's to say?" Doyle said.

Poppy went to room 504 and found the door unlocked. She pushed it open and went in followed by Doyle. "It's warm in here, that's odd. Earlier it was cold. Maybe Jane is moving on now, with Herman."

"Well, I hope they're happy. Unless they both will be haunting the hotel now," Doyle said with a grin.

Poppy kissed him and said, "Yeah, well, I'm not coming back to find out."

*

Chapter 28

Hallsey came back up the stairs and over to Doyle and Poppy. Doyle and Oscar had already put the furniture back in the room so the only thing in the hallway was Herman's wheelchair.

"We're going to take the wheelchair and give it to some organization for the handicapped. It may help another person," Doyle said to Hallsey as he came up.

"That's fine with me. I have no use for it. I'd like to thank you for the kindness you two have shown me. I called the company and told them about

Winfield. They were pleased that the lawsuit was going away. They actually thanked me. I was amazed."

"Roderick, I learned a long time ago that worrying was bad for a person. It doesn't solve anything. So just relax and do your job." Doyle looked at Poppy and said, "Let's get out of this place. I think I've had enough of it."

Poppy was looking around the hallway. "It's still Halloween. Well, it's after midnight, so technically Halloween is over, but I'm pleased that we had a good night. Despite the fire and Herman's death, even if we didn't see the ghost."

"Yes, we had quite a day. Let's go," he said and wheeled the chair to the elevator.

"Are you actually going down in that?" Poppy asked.

"I've looked death in the face, I think I can take a trip into oblivion in this death trap." He entered followed by Poppy and Hallsey. The cage descended creakily and Doyle was grinning and bearing it.

They reached the main floor and exited the cage, much to Doyle's relief. Andrew came up to them.

"Are you leaving?" he asked.

Doyle's Haunting

"We're finished now. I suppose you heard the story of what Herman went through?" Doyle asked him.

"Mr. Hallsey related the story to me that he got from you. So sad for Mr. McNish."

"Was that his last name? We never asked," Doyle said.

"I got to know him when I had to go down into supply for soap to put in the restrooms up here. He was real nice to me and told me he was once a bellhop, too. He never said it was in this hotel."

"Yeah, well, Andrew, don't fall in love with a guest and murder anyone. I think the ghost of the Algonquin is history now. The place doesn't need any more ghosts."

Doyle and Poppy said their goodbyes and went out. Doyle put the chair in the trunk of his Charger and drove back to his apartment.

On the way, Doyle said, "I think we need a couple days of vacation. Maybe a trip to the cabin would be nice."

"I think we both could use that," Poppy replied with a smile.

Bob Moats

~~*~~

Early the next morning Doyle and Poppy entered the office, Doyle pushing the wheelchair. They saw Oscar and Marco standing at Marge's desk.

"Good morning, ghost hunters," Marco said. "Even though you never actually saw the ghost."

"It was a bit of a disappointment," Doyle replied. "But we survived the night. How was crime in the city last night? Arrest any trick or treaters?"

"It was actually quiet. They had me come in for a double shift because they thought we'd need more police on the streets. Luckily, you called and rescued me from having to patrol."

"Is that why you took so long hanging around the hotel?" Doyle laughed. "You didn't want to work?"

"You got it. I did some investigating this morning and found the file from the detective in charge of the murder of Jane's boyfriend. He had a suspicion that Herman may have been a possible suspect. Otherwise, why was he on the roof that night? But the boy was in the hospital barely alive from his fall and then Jane hung herself. The detective just filed the case away and forgot about it. He wasn't the best detective they had back then. I closed the case, so it's done and forgotten."

Doyle's Haunting

"Did you make a copy of Herman's letter?" Poppy asked.

"I've got it," Marge answered. "It's so sad, how he suffered all those years."

"I'm sure he's at peace now. I hope he's with Jane somewhere," Poppy said.

"As long as they don't both haunt the hotel," Oscar said going to his desk.

"Oscar, did you sleep well last night?" Doyle asked his friend.

"By the time I got home, it was after two and I couldn't sleep thinking about everything that happened last night. I may have gotten an hour or two, but I'm dragging today."

"If you don't have a case to go on, why don't you go back home and catch a couple hours sleep?"

"If you don't mind, I may do that," Oscar smiled. "Us old people need our naps. Besides, I have to figure out how to put in a security system to protect my apartment."

"Go ahead and go. If a big crime wave hits, Marge will call you," Doyle said.

Oscar said his goodbyes and left. Doyle turned to Marge and asked, "How did your handing out candy go last night?"

"Very nice, I had just enough candy before the little devils stopped coming. I put the leftovers on your desk, Arthur."

Doyle looked back and saw the bowl with assorted candy. He laughed and said, "Not that I need it, but thanks."

"Do you have any more spooky cases now?" Marco asked.

"No, we're thinking of going up to my cabin for a few days to break it in. I don't need any more demons, Skeeter or hotel ghosts. I just want to sit around the lake and watch Poppy fish. I'm taking her out to buy her a complete fishing outfit."

"She'd look good in waders," Marco laughed.

"I fish in the nude," Poppy said with a smirk.

That stopped Marco. He laughed and said, "I have to go back to work. I'm not like you people who can set your own hours. Some law enforcement has to be on the job protecting the city from criminals. Have a safe trip up north." He left after saying his goodbyes.

Doyle's Haunting

Marge asked, "When are you two going to the cabin?"

"Shortly, we already packed to go. I just wanted to come in and see if there was anything needing my attention. Why don't you call it a day, too?"

"I just got in. I'll relax here and take calls, if we get any," Marge said.

"Whatever you want to do, the office is yours now. Leave when you feel like it. We'll be back in a couple days. Call if anything important comes up."

"I will. Have a nice time." She said.

They walked towards the back door when Doyle stopped.

"What's the matter?" Poppy asked.

"I could swear I left that wheelchair back by the storage area. Now it's up by Oscar's desk."

"Probably a slight slope in the floor, don't make something out of it. Herman's ghost didn't move it. Let's go," she said and pulled him to the door.

They went back out to the car and headed north. Doyle called his sheriff friend, Mike, to let him know they were coming.

"It's quiet here," Mike said through the hands-free setup Doyle had for his phone.

"Good, we need a rest and I have a great story to tell you. Maybe you and your wife can get together with us for dinner?"

"That would be great. I'll let her know. How did Larry treat you over the furniture? I haven't talked to him since he delivered the stuff."

"He did fine. We'll be there in about a half hour. I'll call you later about dinner." They finished and he hung up.

Doyle sat back and put the car on cruise control. "I need to ask one thing."

"What?" she asked.

"Can we not talk about ghosts anymore, except when we tell Mike the story?"

"I'm all for that," Poppy replied and watched out the car window at the leaves of the trees, all colorful now.

THE END

Doyle's Haunting

The Jim Richards books by Bob Moats

(In series order)

For a preview or to purchase a book, go to http://murdernovels.com

Jim Richards Family of Readers

Thanks to the following people who are now part of the Jim Richards Family of Readers. They have read a book or more and enjoyed them. They all volunteered to be included in the list. If you are a fan of the books, send me your full name and you will be included in future books. Send your name to murdernovels@bobmoats.com to be added here and on the website.

* Achim Feifel * Al Norris * Alex Wheatley * Alexandra Delporte-Wilkinson * Amy Tapia * Andrea Bryan * Anne Shepherd * Arianda Sugar * Arlene Markowski * Ashley Augustus * Audra Hall * Barbara Hughes * Barbara Sammons * Barbara Schuler * Barbara Zirger * Beth Donohue Plenskofski * Beth Rosin * Betsy Childress * Beth Gibson * Bill Sandy * Bill Tornquist * Billie-Jo Collie * Boni J Rychener * Candace Larson * Carl Bishopric * Carla Lewis * Carole Henderson * Carolyn Conroy * Carolyn Riddle-Linington * Cassy Bailey * Cathie Turner * Chad Hudson * Charlie Meier * Charlotte L Duran * Cheryl L. Everett * Cindy Ackley Nunn * Cindy Valstad * Connie Bancroft * Corinne Kay O'Daniel * Dana Robbins Chuchran * Dana Wichita * Daniel Kalus * Danielle Monique * Darren Heald * Dave Travers * David Wilkinson * DeAnn Jannereth * Deanna Miller * Deb Breuker Balbo * Debbie Carter * Debbie White * Deborah Fartuch * Deborah Gauze * Deborah Sullivan * Dee King * Denise Freeman * Diana Carver * Dixie Beck * Donna Gould * Donna Thompson * Donny Minter * Doris Kight * Eddie Moore * Eric Walters * Felicia Annette Bradfield * Francine Menor * Gail Chesney *

Doyle's Haunting

Georgiann Minster * George Conner * Greg Colucci * Hayley Rankin * Harold Garcia * Heidi Arnold * Irma Ranee Coy * Jacqueline Moss * Jan Kimball * Janet Lawson * Janice Schneider * Janice Spoor * Jennifer Redmond * Jerry Dornak * Jessica Keown-Belous * Jim Beck * Jo Boguslaw * Jo Turner * Joanne Marie Turner * John Gross * John Peiffer * John Wisbiski * Joseph Wauro * Joyce Stacy * Joyce Trifiletti * Judy Franklin * Judy Travers * Judy Padgett * Julie Heath * Junnahvee Benson * Karen Dahl * Karen Grams * Karen Higham * Karen Kaiser * Karen Meinburg Richwine * Karen Kirkman Parker * Karin Hawkins * Karin Vasvari * Kathleen Donohue Roesing * Kathleen Riddle-Wolfe * Kathy Hinds Moore * Kathy Jones * Kathy Mitchell * Katie Benzler * Kay Burns * Kelly Garcia * Ken Boggs * Keota Rodriguez * Kiera Mccarthy * Kim Estes * Kimberley May * Kitty Stolle * Kristie Sciler * Kirsty Stanton * LaLonnie Scallen * Larry Morris * Leann Parr * Lenora Scales * Leslie Marie Jackson * Linda Bartley Florence * Linda Forester * Linda Ingle Cox * Linda Kennerö * Linda Magill * Lisa Bower * Lisa Keller * Liz Gibson * Lorraine Wiman * Loretta Alexander * Lynda Bowles * Lynette Lawrance * LuAnn Louttit * Manny Rothman * Marcia Gibson DeWitt * Marie Calder * Marlene Bryan * MaryLouise Kramp * Mary Lynn Gross * Megan Atkins * Meghan Hyden * Melissa Wescoat * Melody Cannavan * Michael Carruthers * Michael Dinkens * Michael Vannoy * Michelle Burns-Mitchell * Michelle Pilcher * Micki Potter * Mike Moats * Mimi Baur * Myrna Hecht * Nadine Sutton * Nancy Ellen Sayre * Natalie Quine * Neena Martin * O'Della Wilson * Pat Pollington * Pat Rohn * Patricia Jarmon * Patricia C Trezza * Patrick Barry * Paul Lawrance * Peggy Davis * Phyllis Bassett * Raylene Matheny * Rebecca Collins Besner * Renee Brumley * Reta Hanna * Reta Moats *

Bob Moats

Robert Lenski * Roberta Meister * Roberta Navarro-Harder * Sally Berneathy * Sally Hubler * Sara Swope * Sarah Santos * Satka Nikc * Sharon E. Edwards * Sharon Mangini * Sharon McMillon * Sheena Rawl * Sherry Amstutz * Sherry Tull * Shirley Alvarez * Shirley Davies * Shirley Williams * Stacie Rowe * Stephanie Conner * Steve Cullen * Susan Haughton * Susan Hesse Adams * Susan Salomon * Suzan K Chase * Taisha Cullum * Tamara Moore * Tammy Castleberry * Tammy Lynn Wood * Ted Murphy * Terri Atkins * Terri Creech * Terry Raab * Tonia Rachael Riggs-Williams * Tonya Mann * Travis Fleury-Lopez * Twyla Gawlas * Val Brooks * Walt Munsel * Yvonne Isakson

Thank you to all these wonderful people.

Thank you for purchasing this book. I hope you enjoy it as much as I enjoyed writing it for my faithful readers. Please feel free to email me to tell me what you thought about my stories. I love hearing from the readers. I can be reached at murdernovels@bobmoats.com thanks again!

*